Brandon's request was eloquent and simple and it touched her. April recognized that Brandon wasn't some kid with a hidden agenda. Like her, he was lonely. He also had something buried deep inside his psyche that was painful. She guessed it had to do with the loss of his mother. She wouldn't probe. If he wanted to talk about it, he would.

"I would like that very much," she said. She gazed out to the open sea. A sailboat leaned into the wind against the horizon. "You know, I've watched those boats from the first day I arrived, and I'd love to go sailing on one. Do you think we could do that sometime?"

Turn to the back of this book
for a sneak preview of
Till Death Do Us Part,
the companion to *For Better, for Worse, Forever.*

For Better,
for Worse,
Forever

Lurlene McDaniel

For Better, for Worse, Forever

BANTAM BOOKS

NEW YORK • TORONTO • LONDON • SYDNEY • AUCKLAND

RL 4.7, AGES 012 AND UP

FOR BETTER, FOR WORSE, FOREVER

A Bantam Book / September 1997

ISBN 0-553-57088-9

Published simultaneously in the United States and Canada

Bantam Books are published by Bantam Books, a division of Bantam Doubleday Dell Publishing Group, Inc. Its trademark, consisting of the words "Bantam Books" and the portrayal of a rooster, is Registered in U.S. Patent and Trademark Office and in other countries. Marca Registrada. Bantam Books, 1540 Broadway, New York, New York 10036.

PRINTED IN THE UNITED STATES OF AMERICA

OPM   10   9

To Flo Conner

"He will wipe away every tear from their eyes. There will be no more death or mourning or crying or pain, for the old order of things has passed away."

REVELATION 21:4 (NIV)

For Better,
for Worse,
Forever

1

At the top of the hill, a girl, her red hair gleaming in the sun, stood gazing out at the sea. As she lifted her eyes skyward, she turned and spun in a circle, her arms flung out straight and wide.

She stopped spinning, reached into the pocket of her shorts, and took out a red balloon. She put it to her lips and blew, filling it up so that it rounded out. She tied it off, then reached back into her pocket and pulled out a long thin yellow ribbon. She tied one end securely to the balloon's knotted tail.

As a balmy breeze blew from the sea, she unleashed the ribbon and the balloon flew upward. She shielded her eyes from the glare of the sun and watched as the air current caught the balloon and pulled it so that it rose until it became a tiny red dot lost against the endless blue sky.

Brandon Benedict couldn't believe what he was seeing. A girl—a beautiful girl—with hair so fiery red that it glistened in the sun like sparks from a fire stood shielding her eyes as a red balloon sailed upward into the vibrant blue sky high above the island of St. Croix.

He'd gone hiking alone in the green hills. What an odd thing to discover. She hadn't seen him, so he stayed behind some bushes, out of her line of vision. She appeared to be conducting a private ritual.

Brandon decided not to intrude, but when his heel crushed a dry branch, its loud crack made the girl whirl and catch sight of him. He heard her gasp, then shout, "What do you want?" Her fists were clenched and he thought that she might strike him.

"Nothing."

"Why are you spying on me?"

"I wasn't spying." Her angry gaze bore into him, and he felt defensive.

"Why are you up here?"

He felt his anger rise as he replied, "It's a

free country, you know. I was just out hiking. Sorry if I ruined your day."

Now she looked less angry, more embarrassed. "I thought I was alone."

"And now you will be." He turned and started back down the hill.

"Wait!" she called after him. Her voice was gentler now. "I'm sorry. I didn't mean to yell at you. You just surprised me, that's all."

His irritation vanished and he turned back to her. Her blue eyes were heavy with sadness. He felt it like an electric current. He recognized that sadness. Even now, he could feel the darkness of his own pain, but he shook it off as he smiled. "I'm Brandon Benedict. I live on St. Croix. I hike up in these hills a lot. I had no idea anyone was up here. I didn't mean to scare you."

"My parents have rented that house." She pointed and he saw the white barrel tile of a roof below. "I'm April Lancaster."

"You're renting the Steiner place? I've grown up here. I know most every house and its owners on this side of the island," he explained. "The Steiners were regulars at the Buccaneer Golf Course until Mr. Steiner had a heart attack. They moved back to the

States. I work at the Buccaneer. After school and during summers, I mean. But I guess I'm telling you more than you probably want to know."

She offered a tentative smile. It pleased him immensely. "It's okay. Actually, we've been here three weeks and I haven't met a soul."

"You're kidding! You're so pretty. I—I mean, all you have to do to meet people around here is show up in Christiansted." He waved in the general direction of St. Croix's largest city. "There's nightlife down there."

The veil dropped over her eyes again. "I'm not into partying."

He itched to know what would make such a pretty girl so sad and isolated. "Everything around here is low-key. Even our parties. Where did you come from, anyway?"

"New York. Long Island, actually."

"How long will you be staying?"

She shrugged. "As long as it takes."

"As long as what takes?"

"Forget it," she answered quickly, then added, "we don't have a time limit on our visit. Maybe until the weather turns horrible."

Brandon laughed. "Then you've got a long visit. It's always beautiful here. Summer can get hot, but that'll be months from now." He came closer and saw that her complexion was the color of cream, with the faintest hue of rose across the bridge of her nose and her cheeks. He realized he was gawking and felt self-conscious. "You need to be careful of the sun. It can fry you, even on cloudy days."

"Thanks for the advice."

He was running out of small talk, but he didn't want to walk away from her. "They say too much sun can cause cancer." She gave him an odd, almost amused look he couldn't read. "You're not afraid of cancer?"

"No." Her answer, low and soft, sounded so final that it made him shiver.

"I'm running off at the mouth," he confessed. "I, um, guess I should be going."

"It was nice to meet you," she said politely.

"Look, if you ever want someone to show you the sights—"

"That's all right. I appreciate it, but I'm not looking for company. Nothing personal," she added hastily.

It struck him that she probably had a boyfriend back in New York. A girl as attractive
as April *must* have a boyfriend. "If you
change your mind, I'm in the phone book
under William Benedict. That's my father."

She shook her head. "I won't change my
mind."

Feeling awkward, Brandon turned and
jogged downward, skidding on the rough
terrain but not looking back until he'd come
to the bottom of the hill. Stopping to catch
his breath, he turned for a look. She stood,
small against the blue sky, looking up. He
decided she was searching for the balloon,
and he too gazed up. All he could see were
puffy clouds and a seagull or two. The balloon was gone. He hoped it had gotten to
where she'd wanted it to go. It surprised him
when the idea of heaven crossed his mind.

April scanned the brilliant blue sky until the
brightness made her eyes water. The balloon
was gone. It had been swallowed up. She
wished she could still see it. It represented
her link with Mark. The red balloon had been
her tribute to Mark until the boy had come

along and interrupted her. Brandon. Brandon's face was so different from Mark's. Brandon had sun-streaked brown hair and blue eyes; he was tan, muscular, and robust-looking. Mark, who'd had curly dark brown hair and intense deep brown eyes, had been tall and thin, a victim of cystic fibrosis. Mark was dead and nothing could change that awful reality.

She shivered from the memories. Her mother was probably worried about her by now, so April started down toward the villa where gardens teeming with exotic flowers slashed color along the white stucco walls. Her parents, at the breakfast table, looked up, and her mother asked, relief flooding her face, "Out for a walk?"

"Yes. It's a nice morning."

Her father lowered the fax he'd been reading from his office in Manhattan. April couldn't get used to him in Bermuda shorts and flowered shirts; she'd rarely seen him in anything but a suit, back home. "Hi, princess." A smile split his face. "Hungry? Mango and papaya?" He gestured toward a platter of cut-up tropical fruit.

"Maybe later. I'll be in my room."

As her parents exchanged glances, her mother said, "You should eat something."

"I'm not hungry."

She wasn't in her room for five minutes before her mother knocked, came in, and eased onto the bed, where April sat staring out the window at the sea. "Honey, we should talk."

"I don't want to talk."

"We're concerned about you. It's been months since Mark—"

"I know how long it's been. I don't need you to remind me."

Her mother sighed. "We thought that coming to St. Croix would help."

April bit back her irritation. It wasn't her parents' fault. In fact, they'd tried everything to help her feel better. "Coming here has helped," she said earnestly. "If I'd had to stay in New York, I'd have gone crazy."

"But to us it doesn't seem to have helped. You barely eat. You keep to yourself day in and day out. You never want to go anywhere with us. It's a wonderful island, April. We thought we'd go into town tonight and eat at a Danish restaurant in Christiansted. Fine food."

"You and Daddy go. I really don't want to." Why couldn't her mother leave her alone?

"April, it's not only your depression that worries us. We're fearful about your health too. You are feeling all right physically, aren't you? I mean, you aren't experiencing headaches and not telling us, are you?"

April hardly ever thought about her health these days. It seemed as if the headaches, dizzy spells, blackouts, and six weeks of radiation treatments that she'd had to endure because of the brain tumor had never happened. Or at least, hadn't happened to her. She'd been so focused on Mark, so consumed with his hospitalization and, in spite of his imminent death, her commitment to having a wedding that she'd shoved her own problems aside. "Dr. Sorenson told us the tumor was dormant, and I've no reason to think it isn't," April answered truthfully.

"I know what he *said*, but what matters is how you *feel*."

"I feel fine," April insisted through gritted

teeth. "I mean as fine as a person can feel who watched her fiancé die."

"Oh, honey . . ." Her mother reached for her.

April turned away. "Don't. Please. I don't think I can stand one more tear."

That evening her parents went into town for dinner and April moped around the sprawling house. Far out to sea, she saw a storm brewing, the clouds on the horizon gray and angry looking. She fell asleep on the sofa and in her dreams relived the terrible night at the racetrack. In slow motion, she saw Mark's car strike the bumper of the car in front of him. She saw his car spin out of control, hit the retaining wall, and catch fire. She tried to run onto the track, but in her dream, her feet had taken root in the grandstand and all she could do was watch helplessly.

A roar like flames split the night and she screamed Mark's name. Then she bolted upright, and rain was pelting her face. Wind had toppled a lamp and it had broken on the tile floor. Gasping, sobbing, she stumbled off the sofa and struggled against the wind to shut the French doors. By the time she'd closed them, she was soaked, and rainwater had puddled on the floor and stained nearby furniture.

The tropical squall had moved like quicksilver, sending shards of lightning from the sky to the ground, furious in its intensity. She leaned against the door, watching trees and bushes whip in the dark, watching delicate flowers rip from branches and smear on the glass. And she felt a kinship with the flowers. She knew what it was like to be torn apart and sacrificed to the winds of cruel fate.

2

B randon paced about his room like a caged animal. His father was out of town on business. Not that Brandon cared. They didn't have much to say to each other these days. Brandon flopped on his bed, his hands clasped behind his head, and stared up at the ceiling. It had been a lousy week at school. He'd all but slept through his classes, he'd been so bored. And even though he'd taken on extra hours at his job, he wasn't tired enough to fall into bed so totally exhausted that he could check out. And forget.

He thought about calling his best friend, Kenny, but remembered that Kenny was out with Pam, his red-hot romance of the past few months. Mentally Brandon skimmed his list of other friends and rejected the idea of calling any of them. Truth was, he'd been in such a dark mood for the past five months that nobody wanted to be with him. Even Flo, the girl he'd dated since the previous summer, had dumped him.

"You've got to get over it," she'd said with a toss of her blond head. "Life goes on, Brandon. You can't crawl in the grave with your mother, you know." She'd told him she was sorry, but that she wanted to have fun her senior year, not be tied down to a guy who was so moody.

Brandon sat upright and wandered out of his bedroom and into the kitchen. The place was spotless. His father saw to that. Not at all like the mess his mother had barely maintained when she was alive. He searched through the refrigerator, now well stocked by the housekeeper who came every day, but nothing appealed to him. He slammed the door and hurried out of the room and into the den, where his father kept a bar.

He pawed through the array of bottles. He could have anything he wanted and there was nobody there to police him. He could get stinking drunk. And pass out. Except that was the course his mother had chosen, and look where it had gotten her. He felt like jumping out of his skin. The house was so quiet. So lonely. He missed his mother. Despite the depression that had ruled her life for the previous three years, he missed her and wanted her back. *People don't come back from the dead.*

Brandon knew he had to get out. Go somewhere. Maybe getting lost in a crowd would help. Maybe it wouldn't. All he knew was that he couldn't hang around this house with its ghosts and memories. He grabbed his car keys and bolted out the side door.

The sound of the doorbell startled April. Her parents were out for the evening and they had no friends in St. Croix that she knew of who would drop by. Maybe it was someone up to no good. It occurred to her that she had opened up the house after the storm. Cool tropical air stirred through the French doors, which led to the garden. Anyone could walk in. No need to ring the bell. In New York doors were locked and bolted, and their house in Long Island had an elaborate security system.

The bell chimed again and she went to the door, flipped on the light switch, and saw Brandon Benedict through the clear glass panes of the front door. He waved and smiled. "Remember me?"

"Yes. What do you want?"

He leaned against the doorjamb. "Company."

The way he stood came across as loneliness. His smile was more bravado than happiness. "Um—my parents—" She stopped. Should she admit that she was alone? Yet, if he'd meant to harm her, he could have done so when they were on the hill. Deciding against sending him away, she unlocked the door and opened it. "My parents are out to dinner, but they'll be back soon. You can come in."

"Thanks." He stepped over the threshold, his hands jammed in his pockets. "I know I shouldn't have just popped in on you. You made it clear that you weren't interested in seeing me again, but I was hoping you might change your mind."

She gestured to the sofa in the living room. The two of them sat, and she curled her legs up under her and turned to him. "I didn't mean to be rude. I just haven't been in the mood to meet new people."

"Being nice can be a pain when you'd rather be alone."

"Sounds like the voice of experience speaking. Don't you have friends? I mean from school?"

"My best friend's got a girl who eats up his free time. No time for hanging anymore."

"My best friend, Kelli, is in college out in Oregon. It's a long way off and I miss her. No girl in your life?"

"We broke up. You out of school?"

"I graduated from high school last June; went to New York University for a couple of months, but had to drop out."

Brandon saw shadows in her eyes again. It looked like the raw pain he knew. Something had happened, but he knew better than to ask. He hated it when people prodded him for explanations of his own moodiness. If she wanted to discuss it with him, she would. "I'll graduate this June," he said. It was now mid-February. "Four more months of utter boredom."

"And then?"

He shrugged. "No plans yet."

She was surprised. He reminded her of guys from her high school, and they'd all been planning on college. The guy she'd dated before Mark had even gotten a soccer scholarship. Brandon looked athletic and she told him so.

"I used to play basketball but don't anymore," he said, and she realized there would be no further explanation.

"I guess it is hard to get motivated in a place like St. Croix," she offered. "It's so beautiful all the time. I can't get very enthusiastic about the future myself." She saw no reason to mention Mark and all her reasons for feeling at such loose ends.

"Even though St. Croix is part of the U.S. Virgin Islands, it doesn't feel much like the mainland down here," Brandon said. "We used to visit Miami, but it wasn't much different there than it is down here. Where you're from, there's winter and snow."

"There's snow, all right." Facing the winter after Mark's death had been unbearable. The night breeze brought the perfumed scent of flowers through the open doors, and from far away, she heard the sound of a ship's horn. "The ocean is awesome and I never grow tired of sitting and watching it. Did you know this house has stairs leading down to a cove and its own private beach?"

"I didn't know." Brandon enjoyed looking at April. She was certainly one of the most strikingly pretty girls he'd ever seen. In the lamp's light, her abundant red hair gleamed in a halo around the top of her head. "Have you gone snorkeling yet?"

"Why, no."

He saw interest in her eyes and seized on it. "Then you're missing some of the best that the Caribbean has to offer. Under the sea there's a whole other world. Because the sand bottom's so white, the sun shines down to great depths, where there are coral reefs big as a jungle, and fish the colors of rainbows."

"I've seen pictures taken under the sea in brochures."

"I, um, I could take you sometime. If you'd like to go, that is. I mean, there are plenty of tourist guides that can do the same thing, but because I've grown up here I know underwater areas they've never dreamed about." He paused, seeing the battle wage in her expression between wanting to have such an adventure and keeping to herself. "If you want to."

Her eyes sparkled expectantly for a moment; then the light went out and she dropped her gaze. "Thanks. But I don't think so."

Her standoffishness was maddening, making Brandon itch—all the more determined to know what made her tick. "Well, the offer's open anytime."

She glanced toward the open French doors, looked distracted, then turned back toward him. "You know, maybe it would be better if you weren't here when my folks get home. It will mean hours of explanation if they find you here, and I'm just not up to it."

He stood. "Sure. I know what you mean. But thanks for letting me stop by and talk. It helped."

She puckered her brow. Could just a few friendly words have made a difference for him? Yet he did appear calmer, less agitated than when he'd arrived. "I'm glad. I enjoyed talking to you too."

She followed him to the front door, where he paused. "Remember, on Saturdays I work at the Buccaneer, which is a pretty cool place in itself. If you ever want to drop by for a tour of the place, ask for me at the pro shop."

She agreed, although she believed she never would, and told him good night.

Once Brandon was gone, April couldn't concentrate on the book she'd been reading before his arrival. There was something about him . . . something lonely and full of longing that she couldn't get out of her thoughts. She'd seen it in his eyes. She'd been made aware of such things through her association with Mark. His CF had isolated him and set him apart from his peers all his life. She remembered his telling her about being ostracized and longing to be a part of "regular" life. Her own illness had set her apart too. Except for Kelli, her friends couldn't relate to a girl with a brain tumor. Not that anyone could see it! It was just that once they knew, everything was different. Guys hadn't been able to handle it either. Not that it had mattered in the long run, because it had opened the door for her relationship with Mark. Still, she knew firsthand what loneliness felt like.

Brandon's visit had brought her own loneliness into sharp focus. Only a few months before, she'd been planning her wedding and looking forward to spending the rest of her life with Mark. She hugged the book to her chest, suddenly missing Mark with an intense yearning. Tears gathered in her eyes. She fought against them, but in the end, they won the battle. *Mark! Mark!* She missed him so much.

April went to bed early and pretended to be sleeping when her parents returned. She kept her eyes closed when her mother peeked inside her room, knowing that she was too old to be tucked in, and her mother too involved with her only daughter not to do so.

The next morning, she went out to breakfast, sat down at the table awash in warm tropical sunlight, and said, "Dad, you told me you'd rent me a car so that I could drive around the island when I felt like it. Is your offer still open?"

Her parents exchanged glances. "Of course. But why not let your mother and me drive you around? We wouldn't mind, and besides, driving these roads can be confusing. In the Virgin Islands they drive on the left-hand side of the road."

"I'd rather be by myself," April said. "I'd like to explore, and don't worry, I can drive on the left-hand side just as easily as I can on the right."

"But—" her mother started.

"It's all right, Janice." Hugh Lancaster interrupted his wife's protest. "If that's what April wants, then that's what she'll have. What would you like to rent?"

"How about a Jeep?"

He nodded. "A Jeep it will be."

3

April downshifted and the Jeep wound its way along the coastal highway. Her father had taken her the very next morning into the city of Christiansted, where she'd chosen a black Jeep with a canvas top and zippered sides, all of which she'd removed before driving away. Armed with maps and cautions from her parents, she'd headed east, repeating to herself her mother's anxious warning, "Remember, stay left. Stay left."

Wind whipped through her hair as she bounced along the curving highway, rounding bends in the road to glimpse the jewel-blue Caribbean, an occasional rocky cliff, and lush green distant hills. The sun beat down on her arms and shoulders, and the intoxicating smell of salt air mingled with the sweet aroma of flowers. The roads were few on the island and now, in the height of tourist season, not heavy with traffic. She gripped the wheel and stepped on the accelerator as she remembered when Dr. Sorenson had said that despite weeks of radiation treatments, the tumor entrenched in her cerebellum and brain stem had not responded by shrinking as hoped. He was so, so sorry. There was little else medical science could do for her.

Understanding her anguish at the time, Mark had taken her out to a deserted airstrip and told her to drive as fast and as hard as she wanted. And she had forced his fine old car to its optimum speed and experienced the dangerous but exhilarating balance between control and oblivion. It had been a gift that only Mark could have given her, because he was the only one who understood what it was like to live one's life with the ever-present specter of death.

Mark would have loved St. Croix. He would have sped along the back roads and climbed trails where only four-wheel-drive vehicles ventured. They would have had such a good time together. A mist of tears clouded her eyes and she slowed down the Jeep.

She glanced to one side and saw a large sign: THE BUCCANEER. On impulse, she spun the wheel of the car and drove through the gateway and down a sloping road across acres of rolling green land. The edges of a golf course lay on her right, and far back, on a bluff overlooking the sea, stood a sprawling clubhouse and hotel. She parked in the lot and walked out on a terrace set with tables and chairs. A hostess asked, "Do you have a lunch reservation?"

April cleared her throat and smiled nervously. She had no business being there. "Actually, I was looking for your pro shop."

The hostess directed her there, and April hurried out onto the splendid grounds of the luxury resort, down a tiled path, to the shop. Once inside, she asked for Brandon, then busied herself among the clutter of golf paraphernalia. She chided herself, saying that what she was doing was stupid. She had no real reason to see Brandon. She hoped he wasn't there, that this was a Saturday he didn't work. The door opened and she turned to face him across a rack of golf shirts. His face, damp with sweat, broke into a large grin. "I don't believe it! You came to see me!"

She had to laugh at his genuine astonishment. "I was just driving by and saw the sign. I didn't even know if you'd be here."

"I've been here since six A.M. We open early because golfers like to start before it gets hot. I'm about to take a lunch break. Want to eat with me?"

She wasn't hungry, but since she'd come this far and knew she couldn't leave easily, she answered, "Maybe a salad."

He took her back to the terrace restaurant, ordered and had the food packed in Styrofoam containers, then led her down a winding walkway to a sandy beach area. Hotel guests were sunning themselves and playing in the calm waters. He pulled a small table and two chairs around an alcove of rocks to an isolated strip of sand no larger than a good-sized back porch. "Since the tide's out, we can sit here," he said, planting the chair firmly in the wet sand. "It's private."

She removed her sandals, allowing warm

water to lap over her feet. He sat across from her so that he was framed in blue sky and bright turquoise ocean. His tanned face glowed and his hair looked golden, streaked by the sun. "I'm starving," he said, flipping open his container and lifting out a mammoth hamburger.

Watching Brandon wolf down his meal reminded her of all the times she'd eaten with Mark. But, of course, Mark had had to take pills before every meal because of his CF. She thought of "their" special restaurant and of "their" table tucked in the corner.

"What's funny?" he asked. "You were smiling just then. Have I got mustard smeared on my face?"

Self-conscious, she looked down at her salad. "I was just remembering something, that's all. Nothing important."

"I'll be honest," he said between bites. "I never thought I'd see you again."

"Me neither."

"I'm glad you changed your mind. Why *did* you change your mind?"

"I didn't know I needed a reason."

"My charming personality?" he offered with an infectious grin.

"Certainly that was part of it." She returned his smile. A gull swooped low over the water behind him. "I was knocking around the island."

"And you thought, 'Wonder what old Brandon's up to? Maybe I should go see the geek.'" His joking tone reminded her of Mark's.

"Actually, I was . . . lonely." She kept her gaze on the gull, unable to meet Brandon's. She hadn't meant to tell him that.

He leaned back in his chair and searched her face thoughtfully. "I figured something was up with you. I've seen you twice and you looked sad both times." She didn't respond, so he continued. "I've been lonely myself, so I know how it feels."

"Everybody's been lonely."

"But you don't have to be," he said. "April, St. Croix is a small place. Everybody knows everybody else, especially those of us who grew up here. Tourists come through all the time, and sometimes the locals hit it off with some of them. We know that the person is going to leave. That's a given. But we still have a good time together while

we can, as long as the person is on the island . . ."

She understood what he was trying to tell
her—that he would take her under his wing
with no strings attached. "Like a baby-
sitter?"

"You're no baby," he declared, appraising
her in a way that made her pulse flutter. "No.
As a friend. This wouldn't be only for you.
You see, I could use a friend myself."

"There are plenty of tourists who would
jump at the chance to be your friend, Brandon."

"But I don't want just anybody. I'd like it
to be you."

The way he kept looking at her made her
feel even more self-conscious. An inner voice
asked, *What are you doing?* Suddenly she
saw that she was acting flirty, and she was
instantly ashamed. She struggled to stand,
but the wet sand had sucked around the legs
of the chair so that she couldn't move it. "It's
really getting late. I've got to go and you've
got work."

"Don't go yet." Instantly Brandon was beside her, taking her arm so that she wouldn't

fall backward. His touch felt warm, and she pulled away as if it had burned her.

"I have to," she insisted.

"I'd like to see you again. Can I call you? Make a date? I have classes until two, but I'm free evenings. I could show you around St. Croix. Maybe take you over to St. Thomas or St. John."

"I—I don't think so." Despite being in a wide-open space, April felt hemmed in and claustrophobic. "I really have to go now." She grabbed her sandals and backed away. "Thanks."

"Call me here if you change your mind," he said to her as she ducked around the edge of the rocks and fled up the beach toward the parking lot where her Jeep was parked. With her heart hammering, April turned on the engine and shot up the road to the highway, where she forgot the rule about staying in the left-hand lane and almost had a head-on collision.

Jerking the car back into its proper lane, April sped toward the hills and the safety of the villa. She never should have stopped to see Brandon. Not because she wasn't attracted to him, but because she was. And because she kept thinking about another guy who'd wanted to date her but whom she'd rejected at first—Mark. Until he'd won her over with his winsome smiles and caring love and swept her heart away. But now Mark was gone and she couldn't bring him back, and she couldn't start with someone else.

She floored the accelerator and raced toward home, memories chasing her like the wind.

"Did you have a good time exploring?"

Her mother's question cut through April's semiconscious state. She'd hurried home, put on her bathing suit, and gone down to the private beach for a swim. The surf felt warm as bathwater, the white sand bottom soft as velvet. She'd swum and floated to exhaustion, and had finally gone to the beach chair, where she'd slathered herself with sun cream, stretched out, and dozed, hoping to shut off her thoughts. Her mother had come down, bringing a pitcher of cool lemonade. "It was all right," April answered.

Her mother dragged another chair closer. "Tell me about it."

"Nothing to tell. I drove around, that's all."

She heard her mother sigh. "April, I can't stand this noncommunication between us. I know you're hurting, but we used to talk all the time. Now you hardly speak to me. Can't you tell how this is upsetting me? Don't you even care?"

Guilt mixed with irritation, yet April knew her mother was right. Her parents had done plenty for her and she'd shut them out. Just months before, she and her mother had been knee-deep in wedding plans; they'd discussed everything. April struggled to sit upright. "I'm sorry."

"You don't have to be sorry. Just *talk* to me. I love you. I want to help."

"Nothing can help. I can't get on top of this, Mom. I start to feel better and then, *pow,* it hits me like a wall. I miss Mark so much." She took a deep breath. "And every time some guy so much as looks at me, I want to run in the other direction."

Her mother poured April a glass of lemonade, and gulls swooped over the sea, flinging their lonely cries against the sunset-colored sky. "St. Croix is a paradise. It's romantic and makes you want to be with somebody you care about. I understand that."

"But how can I? I feel so guilty to even be thinking about such things."

"I know," her mother said. "I can see it on your face. You feel guilty because you're alive and Mark isn't. And because you want to go on living, as you should."

4

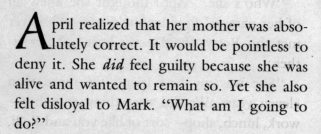

April realized that her mother was absolutely correct. It would be pointless to deny it. She *did* feel guilty because she was alive and wanted to remain so. Yet she also felt disloyal to Mark. "What am I going to do?"

Her mother put her arm around April's slumped shoulders. "Let me tell you a story."

April nodded, still feeling as if she were betraying Mark.

"You know all that your father and I went through to have you. Years of trying to get pregnant and disappointment after disappointment, fertility drugs, and finally going to Europe for in vitro fertilization. Which is why you're an only child. I couldn't do all that again. You're all we ever wanted. You're perfect."

"And then I got a brain tumor when I was five. So much for perfection."

Her mother squeezed her affectionately. "But the tumor was arrested, at least for a time. But what I want to tell you about concerns all those years I tried to get pregnant . . . and about my friend Betsy."

"Who's she?" April thought she knew all of her parents' friends. She'd not only never met this Betsy, she'd never heard of her either.

"She was my best friend for more than eleven years. We did everything together—work, lunch, shop—sort of like you and Kelli, except we were older, mid-twenties to thirties. And we were both trying to have a baby. It helped going through all the frustration and disappointment with another woman. Men can't really grasp the trauma a woman experiences when she wants to get pregnant but can't."

Her mother plucked up a seashell and cradled it in the palm of her hand. "Anyway, at one point Betsy stopped talking to me. She just pulled away and I couldn't figure out why. I begged her to tell me what was wrong. Had I done something to offend her? It was sheer torment for me. Then one day I heard from a mutual friend that Betsy was pregnant. I rushed to her and asked if it was true. It was. And I asked why she hadn't told me. And she said because she hadn't wanted to hurt me. She felt guilty, April, because she had something she knew I desperately wanted."

April heard the emotion in her mother's voice and realized that even now, years later, the event still affected her. "So what happened?"

"I told her I was happy for her, and I was. But I felt so betrayed because she hadn't confided in me. It did irreparable harm to our friendship. She couldn't believe that I could rejoice with her, that I wouldn't be jealous and depressed about it." Her mother paused. "So why am I telling you this? Because you're going through much the same thing. You're alive and Mark isn't. You think he would somehow be disappointed in you if you allow yourself to have fun or date another boy. But from what I know about

Mark, that simply isn't true. No more than my being petty and angry about Betsy's pregnancy would have been true all those years ago.

"Mark understood. He knew what the odds of his dying before you were, even if the wreck had never occurred."

Her mother was right again; Mark had told April as much before their engagement. He had not expected to outlive her. "What are you saying to me?"

"I'm saying it's all right for you to be happy again. Give yourself permission to enjoy your life. To date if you want. To have a good time. It's what Mark would have wanted. And if you'll search your heart, you'll see that I'm telling you the truth. Mark loved you. Now you must honor his love by living, not merely existing."

"But I—"

Her mother interrupted. "Nobody knows how much time she has to live, April. You could have just as easily died before Mark. In an accident . . . anything."

April noted that her mother hadn't said "a relapse." But of course, that was such a real possibility that perhaps there was no need to state it. April shuddered. She didn't want to die. The realization almost took her breath away. But if that feeling didn't make her disloyal, what did it make her?

"Don't you think Mark would have missed you if something had taken you away from him?" her mother continued.

"Sure he would have missed me."

"Wouldn't you have wanted him to feel happy again?"

"You know I would."

"Then stop feeling guilty and start enjoying every day you have to live."

Long after her mother had gone up to the house, April sat staring out at the sea, now calm and flat. The sky was deepening to shades of mauve. Far out against the horizon, a sailboat looked dead in the water. She identified with the boat. She felt limp. She longed for a new breeze, a fresh wind to come into her life and blow away the clouds of despair. She hungered to feel as alive as she had when she'd been with Mark. Was her mother right? While she couldn't have Mark again, was it possible to have something to give her life new meaning?

April decided to give herself permission to get out more and spend more time with her family. When her parents went to restaurants and museums, she accompanied them. They flew to St. Thomas for a day of shopping and antique hunting. She took long drives in her Jeep up into the rain forests of St. Croix and onto the far side of the island to the city of Frederiksted, passing abandoned sugar mills from the island's early history.

She passed the Buccaneer many times, but she never went in to see Brandon. She honestly believed she didn't need the complication of him in her life. She was strolling past shops in downtown Christiansted one afternoon, looking for a gift for Kelli's upcoming birthday, when she heard someone call her name. She turned to see Brandon hurrying toward her. Against her will, her heart gave a little leap. She pasted a smile on her face and braced for the encounter.

"I thought that was you," he said, jogging up. "I mean that red hair of yours is like a stoplight. How've you been? I haven't seen you in a while."

She heard the admonishment in his tone. "I've been around," she told him. "Busy." Even to her ears it sounded lame.

But his grin was quick, forgiving. "Well, now that we meet again, could I buy you an ice-cream cone? That shop across the street has tons of flavors."

The air felt humid and sticky. Ice cream would taste good. "All right," she said, offering him a smile.

Inside the pink-and-white ice-cream parlor, the air was cool and smelled of peppermint and chocolate. They chose different flavors and settled in at a small round table next to the picture window where sun beamed through the glass. "So what's kept you busy?" he asked.

"My parents."

He made a face. "It doesn't sound very exciting."

"I have cool parents. How about you?"

Immediately he stiffened. "My dad and I don't get on too well."

She licked the ice cream, savoring the sweetness. "And your mom?"

"She's dead."

His statement sounded so stark that she gasped. "I'm sorry."

He licked his cone in silence, offering no other explanation.

April cast about for something else to say, something to change the subject. The clock on the wall gave her the opening. "I thought you said you had school on weekdays until two."

"I didn't feel like going today. I skipped."

"Do you have to work?"

"Yeah, but not until three." He leaned back in his chair and stretched out his long legs. "I wanted to come see you but I didn't think you'd open the door for me."

"Look, Brandon—"

"It's okay," he interrupted. "But I want to explain something." She nodded politely, and he continued. "I got to thinking about it and I realized that you've finished high school and I haven't. I figure you don't want to be seen with some local high-school jerk. I'm really eighteen and I should have gradu-ated last June, same as you, but don't go thinking I'm some kind of dumb dork. You see, I had a rough year and I ended up missing too many days, so the administration said I had to repeat most of my senior year. I could have taken a test and gone straight into college. But I, um, I decided to hang back and graduate a year late."

His story surprised her. She suspected there was plenty he wasn't telling her. She wasn't about to dig it out of him either. The less she knew, the easier it would be not to become involved with him. "I didn't have much use for high school by the time graduation rolled around," she told him. "But I was glad I finished. You did what was right for you. And, by the way, I've never thought of you as some high-school jerk."

By now they were both through with their ice cream. "Look, would you like to take a walk on the beach with me? We can go over to the resort, and then I'll be close to my job." He stood and held out his hand. "Please."

She couldn't say no—didn't really want to—so she followed him outside, where they got into their separate cars and drove to the Buccaneer. Once there, they parked and he took her out onto the grounds. The tropical sun beat down and sprinklers arced over the golf course, tossing jewel-like drops of water over the grass. He led her into a forest garden where huge multicolored hibiscus and bright-orange bird-of-paradise flowers grew in well-tended beds. Inside the garden the air felt cooler, and sun-dappled leaves shaded the winding pathways. "I'll never get over how pretty everything is in St. Croix," she said.

Brandon stopped, peered down at her, and, touching the ends of her hair, said, "Yes. I agree. Things *are* more beautiful here."

Her heartbeat accelerated as she caught his message in his eyes. "So where does this path lead?"

"Come. I'll show you."

She followed, and minutes later the path led out of the garden and onto a sunny lawn. There she saw a latticed gazebo, painted white and trimmed with satin ribbons and cascades of white flowers. "How beautiful," she exclaimed.

"We must have just missed the party," Brandon said. He stooped and picked up grains of rice and wild birdseed and tossed them playfully into the air.

"What is this place?"

"It's the wedding chapel. People come from all over the world to be married here."

5

Her heart thudded, and reality crashed in on her. "Can we go somewhere else?"

Brandon looked surprised. "There's no place prettier than here."

"But I don't want to be here." April spun and hurried back up the path into the garden. The flowers, which only minutes before had been breathlessly beautiful to her, now seemed waxen and surreal.

"Wait!" she heard Brandon call. He ran up behind her and caught her arm. "Don't run off. What's wrong? What's happened? I thought you'd like the place. You said St. Croix was perfect and this is one of the prettiest spots on the island."

He must think she was crazy. Her hands trembled, and her knees felt rubbery. The sight of the wedding chapel had opened a wound on her heart that left her reeling and grief-stricken. "Which way to the beach?" she asked, struggling to hold back tears.

"This way." He took her quickly out of the garden, across rolling manicured grass, and down to the shoreline, where the gentle waves rolled onto the sand.

There she stopped and breathed in great gulps of sea air, calming her racing heart. She kicked off her sandals and began to walk along the shore. The water washed over her footprints, blurring them. Brandon walked beside her, not speaking, allowing her the time she needed to gather her composure. She owed him an explanation but wasn't sure how to begin. "I'm sorry, Brandon. I didn't know that was going to happen. I was caught off guard."

"Exactly what *did* happen?"

"Memories," she whispered. "Just when I think they'll never come back, they do."

Again he kept silent.

She said, "My parents brought me to St. Croix to help me get over something. You see, back home, I knew this guy . . . we were very close."

"I knew it!" Brandon stopped walking. "I knew you were too good-looking to not have a boyfriend."

She turned to face him as the waves washed sand out from under her bare feet. "He was more than my boyfriend. Mark was my fiancé."

A somber look crossed Brandon's face. "Oh."

"But he's dead."

He looked jolted and his face went pale. "How . . . ?"

"Have you ever heard of cystic fibrosis?" She told him slowly, haltingly, about Mark and his disease, his love of racing cars, his accident. "He would have made it—the crash wasn't that bad—if it hadn't been for the CF. In the end, it won."

Brandon listened intently. She couldn't read what he was thinking, but she knew her story had affected him because it showed on his face. "Life stinks!"

"But we can't change how life turns out," she said. "Mark didn't deserve to have CF and he didn't deserve to die so young. After he was gone, I hated being in New York without him."

"So you came here."

"Winter up there is awful . . . the sky all gray and cold. Bare trees." She shivered. "Everywhere I went reminded me of him. Last June, when I graduated, my father wanted us all to go on a family vacation, but at the time I was involved with Mark and I didn't want to leave. Once he was gone . . ." She shrugged, leaving the sentence unfinished. "I love it here . . . the ocean and all."

"What were you doing that day I first saw you up on the hill? It had something to do with Mark, didn't it?"

"CF robs a person of his breath, so blowing up a balloon was a pretty big deal for Mark. He used to blow up balloons for me as a present. Sometimes he'd tuck little notes inside. This time, *I* blew up a balloon for him, and I sent it up into the sky on the chance that he was up there, looking down. I wanted him to know I was thinking about him. And that I loved him."

"Mark was a very lucky guy to have had you."

"No, I was the lucky one." Tears brimmed in her eyes. "We were right in the middle of planning the wedding when Mark died. Seeing that wedding chapel . . . well, it brought everything back."

"I'm sorry."

"You had no way of knowing." She turned to face him, smiling tentatively. "But you're right, it is beautiful."

Brandon shifted from foot to foot. "Now that I know about you and Mark, it explains some things to me. I understand that you might not want some guy pressuring you and coming on to you. But let me be honest. I still would like to see more of you. Nothing heavy," he added quickly. "But I do know every inch of this island and most of the surrounding water. If you'll let me, I'd like to be your friend. I'd like to take you around and show you my island."

His request was eloquent and simple and it touched her. She recognized that Brandon wasn't some kid with a hidden agenda. Like her, he was lonely. He also had something buried deep inside his psyche that was painful. She guessed it had to do with the loss of his mother. She wouldn't probe. If he wanted to talk about it, he would.

"I would like that very much," she said.

She gazed out to the open sea. A sailboat leaned into the wind against the horizon. "You know, I've watched those boats from the first day I arrived, and I'd love to go sailing on one. Do you think we could do that sometime?"

A dark expression crossed his face, prompting her to ask, "You do sail, don't you?"

"We have a boat. A nice one, but it's in dry dock."

"Repairs? Painting?"

He shook his head. The gloom in his eyes passed and he gave a quick grin. "We'll rent a little boat, big enough for two. I'll teach you how to sail it. How to tack and swing the sail about without knocking yourself into the water."

"I'd like to learn."

A beeping sound interrupted them, and Brandon glanced down at his watch. "My cue to go to work," he said, flipping off the miniature alarm. "I'd like to call you."

She'd enjoyed the afternoon and realized she wanted to see him again. "Sure."

He offered to walk her to her car, but she told him, "You go on. I'm going to walk on the beach awhile longer."

"Talk to you soon," he called, and jogged off toward the golf course.

She watched him, gave a deep sigh, and whispered, "I hope this is okay with you, Mark."

By the time Brandon pulled into his driveway, night had fallen. The lights were on inside the sprawling house, which meant that his father was home, returned from one of his many business trips. Brandon couldn't say he was glad. The less he had to do with his father the better. He went into the kitchen through the garage and saw his father sitting at the breakfast bar, nursing a drink over a half-eaten sandwich.

"Where have you been?"

"Working." Brandon crossed to the refrigerator, every nerve in his body tingling.

"I called the Buccaneer at five and they told me you were gone."

"Well, your source was wrong. At the last minute Doug decided the grounds crew needed to mulch the garden near the sixteenth hole. So that's what I did."

"What about your schoolwork? Or are you

going to take yet another pass at your senior year?"

Low blow, Brandon thought, but he ignored the barb. "I didn't have any homework." No need to mention that he'd skipped school that day.

"When I come home after a week away on the job, I expect to see you. I wanted us to have dinner together."

"It was never important to you before," Brandon shot back. "Mom and I ate by ourselves half my life."

"You watch your mouth. I was trying to earn a living."

Brandon glared at his father. "Well, now you have all the time in the world."

Rage crossed his father's face, and Brandon knew he'd stepped over the line. He didn't care. Why should he spare his father's feelings? "You think I chose to leave the two of you alone so much? You think you know so much about taking care of a family? About making sure they have the things they want? Well, I've got news for you, Brandon, you don't know a thing!"

Brandon fished in his pocket and pulled out his car keys. "I know I'm out of here."

His father stood, tipping over the kitchen stool. "You do not have my permission to leave."

"I didn't ask for it."

"You can't leave until I say so."

His father took a step forward, but Brandon met his challenge. "Watch me."

"Your car—"

"Is mine. It belonged to my mother and she left it to me. And I pay for the gas and insurance."

His father raised his hand as if to slap Brandon. Brandon didn't flinch. His father sagged against the counter and buried his face in his hands. "I—I don't want to fight with you, son."

"Too late," Brandon said. He slammed the kitchen door, got into the car, and screeched out of the garage. But he stopped at the end of the driveway. It was after ten and he really didn't have anyplace to go. Why did it have to be this way between him and his father? Why did they always end up in a yelling match?

Brandon bowed his forehead until it touched the steering wheel gripped between his hands. His heart pounded crazily and his body shook. Of course, the questions were pointless. He knew *why*. There was just nothing he could do about it. He turned his roiling thoughts to April and immediately felt calmer. She understood what it was like to lose somebody you loved. But she didn't understand what it was like to lose somebody the way he had lost his mother.

Brandon turned off the car's engine and leaned back against the seat. Exhaustion overwhelmed him. Tropical night air blew through the lowered car windows, tantalizing him with the familiar scent of gardenia. His mother had worn that same fragrance. He waited at the end of the driveway until all the lights went off inside the house. Until the night sounds from the surrounding jungle had blotted out the sounds of neighborhood dogs, TVs, and moving cars. Until he was positive his father was asleep and he could steal inside, alone and unnoticed.

6

The next morning April told her parents about meeting Brandon. Not about their very first meeting, atop the hill, or about the second one, when he came to the house, but about the third. She embellished, saying that she'd gotten lost and he'd come to her rescue at the Buccaneer. "He seems nice, and I think you'll like him. He wants to show me around St. Croix."

Her father poured coffee for the three of them. "I can't say I blame him. You are the prettiest girl on the island."

April rolled her eyes.

"Do you want to see him?" her mother asked.

Their gazes met, and April thought back to

their conversation that one afternoon on the beach. "Yes, I'd like to see him. I'd like to have him show me the island."

"We can show you the island," her father declared.

"Don't be a wet blanket, Hugh," her mother said. "We're just parents. April needs to be with someone her own age. Besides, now that you're commuting back and forth to New York, you'll only be here on the weekends. What's she supposed to do during the weekdays?"

"I only go every other week," he corrected her, then leaned toward April. "You sure you don't want to go to New York with me?"

April shook her head. "I like it here."

"We'll both go with you on one of the trips," her mother offered. "In the meantime, I've been thinking of spending a few days in the British Virgin Islands."

The British counterpart wasn't far away, but to go would mean spending several days there. "Maybe later this summer," April hedged. "Of course, you can go if you want. I'll be fine by myself."

She caught their reluctance to go off and

leave her to fend for herself in their glances at each other. It bothered her that they were so overprotective, but she wasn't in any mood to start an argument about it. Fortunately, the phone rang just then, and her father answered and handed it over to her. "I'll bet it's that Brandon."

It was. She quickly made plans, and later that afternoon when he came, she made sure her parents met him. Once in his car, she said, "Sorry about that," referring to the numerous questions her father had asked.

He laughed. "Do I still have arms and legs? I thought your father was going to bite them off."

"They can't help it. It came with their parenting lease." She remembered apologizing to Mark for her family's possessiveness of her, but he had known about her health problems and made allowances. Brandon did not know.

"They care," Brandon said. "It's no big deal. Forget it."

"So where are we going?"

"Have you driven up into the rain forest?"

"Once. But I was on my way someplace else."

"Then that's where we're headed."

He drove into the hills, where tangled undergrowth and thick tree trunks lined the sides of the road. Brandon slowed, pulled off to one side, took April's hand, and led her into the dense foliage. The air felt damp and heavy. Her hair stuck to the back of her neck. She heard a breeze rustle through the tree branches high above but couldn't feel it. The trees absorbed it, like sponges sucking up water. "It's so quiet," she said. "I feel as if we should be whispering."

"It's not so quiet," he said. "Listen."

She heard a faint clacking sound.

"That's the seedpods of Tibet trees. They're called 'mother's tongue.'"

She giggled. "Yes, I recognize the voice."

Next he took her to an artesian village where wood-carvers were busy shaping everything from small animals to large pieces of furniture from pieces of mahogany. April pronounced it "major cool."

Brandon bought her several hand-carved combs, which she immediately used to sweep up her hair and secure it off her neck. He also bought her a hand-carved necklace.

"You shouldn't buy me so much."

"You're fun to buy for," he said, remembering the many small gifts he'd bought for his mother in an effort to lift her spirits when dark depression overtook her. "Here, let me fasten it for you."

He stepped behind her and slipped the necklace around her neck. He was struggling with the clasp when he noticed the line of blue dots at the base of her neck. "Who's been drawing on you?"

She stiffened. "What do you mean?"

"There's this pattern of little blue specks on your skin. Sort of like blue freckles."

She jerked the combs from her hair and let it tumble down around her shoulders. She knew what he'd seen—the tiny tattoos the radiologist had made when she'd begun her radiation treatments the year before. But she couldn't tell him; she couldn't. "Birthmarks," she fibbed. "Someone in the family was a blueblood."

He eyed her, uncertain as to his response. The dots were too orderly, too mathematical and precise to be a random pattern from birth. Yet her message in her attempt to make a joke about them was plain enough: Don't ask. "Gee, I thought for a minute you'd been abducted by aliens."

"I was, but I escaped," she said, glad he didn't press her for a serious answer.

"Now that I've seen your funny blue freckles, you may as well put your hair back up," he told her. "It's hot."

She complied, lifting her hair and fastening it with the wooden combs, careful to face him as she worked. "Now where?" she asked, pretending the previous conversation had never happened.

"I know where there's a waterfall, but we'll have to hike to it. You want to go?"

She did.

She followed him along a partially hidden trail, the sound of falling water growing in intensity. "It's not much farther," Brandon said.

Just when she was certain they'd never get there, Brandon moved aside overhanging brush and she saw a clearing. Beyond it she saw the waterfall tumbling from a height of rocks and into a stone-littered pool where the water was so clear that she could see all the way to the bottom. Where the falls hit, water boiled up white and frothy, like a milk shake. The air felt cool and moist with water droplets.

"Look," April cried, pointing. "I see a rainbow." Ribbons of color arched over the tumbling water.

"It's the way light hits water droplets," Brandon said.

"Is not. It's fairy dust."

He laughed. "Come on. Take off your shoes, we'll sit on that rock."

She followed him out onto a jutting rock shelf where water lapped against the cool stone. She dangled her feet and sucked in her breath. "It's cold."

"It's right out of a spring. Nice, huh?"

"Very nice. Thanks for bringing me."

"I discovered it one day when I was hiking. I've never brought anybody here to see it with me."

April realized that in his way, he was telling her that she was special to him. She wasn't sure how she felt about his veiled compliment, so she changed the subject. "You hike a lot, don't you?"

"The whole island is only twenty-three miles long, and when you've lived here as long as I have, you get to know it pretty well."

"How long have you lived here? And why?"

"I've been here since I was seven. My father's in importing and exporting. He travels a lot, and this is a good jumping-off place to South America and the rest of the Caribbean."

"So you and your mom spent a lot of time by yourselves?"

At the mention of his mother, April saw him draw away. "Yeah. We did. But she never liked it as much as I did. She was Danish and because the Danish settled this place you'd have thought she'd like it, but she missed her family back in Europe. And Dad was gone so much."

April was on the verge of asking him what had happened to his mother when a wild bird, brilliant with red and yellow plumage, swooped down from one of the trees with a raucous cry. One of its red tail feathers fluttered into the pool, where it floated and bobbed.

"Look! It's beautiful."

"Do you want it?"

"Can you reach it?" It seemed out of his reach and was headed toward the frothy swirl at the foot of the falls. Once there, it would be sucked under and lost.

Brandon grinned and stood. "If you want it, it's yours." He dove headfirst into the pool.

"You'll freeze," she shouted with a laugh.

He surfaced, swam confidently, and captured the feather. He ceremoniously placed it between his teeth and swam back to her, then pulled himself up onto the rock and, dripping wet, bowed with a flourish, presenting her with the feather prize.

She stood and clapped. "You look like a pirate."

His grin dazzled her. "The feather's magic. Make a wish and whatever you want is yours."

She took it, her mind spinning. There was too much to wish for. "I wish . . . I could fly just like the bird that lost this feather."

Mischief danced in his eyes. "You can. Have you ever been parasailing?"

"Are you sure I can do this?" April stood on the back of a speedboat, nibbling nervously on her bottom lip and watching Brandon and two men from the Buccaneer. One was a driver for the boat, and the other was strapping her into a harness that was attached to a huge parachute. It lay in the sea like a flattened orange jellyfish, lines and ropes slack.

"It's a no-brainer," Brandon assured her. "You're going to love this." He'd picked her up the next afternoon and driven her to the resort, where he'd paid the two men on duty to take her parasailing.

"It's not my brains I'm worried about," she muttered. "It's my body being smashed into the ocean and turning into shark bait."

The parasailing instructor laughed heartily. "You'll do just fine, little lady. I haven't lost a client yet." She listened as he instructed her, feeling both apprehensive and excited. "Just hang on and let the boat do the work. You'll have about fifteen minutes in the air, and then I'll reel you in like a big fish." He gestured to a mammoth reel mounted on the back of the boat that held a rope from her harness. The parachute, in turn, was tied to the metal frame of the harness. "Ready?" he asked.

She lied, telling him, "Yes." The driver

pushed the throttle forward. As the boat gathered speed, she saw the parachute begin to fill and rise and felt her body lift gently off the deck. A thrill shot through her as she rose higher and higher, like a human kite adrift on the wind. Below, the boat looked toylike, the vivid blue ocean bright as sapphire. The noise of the boat's engine faded too, and the sound of the wind filling the nylon parachute reminded her of a sheet flapping in a stiff breeze.

She could see for miles and miles, islands surrounded by sugar-sand beaches, green rolling hills, and more ocean, vast and blue and stretching into infinity. *So this is how an eagle feels,* she thought. *This is what flying with wings would be like.* Joy bubbled up inside her, all fear and apprehension gone, blown away by the wind and melted by the warmth of the sun. The vastness of creation, the beauty of sea and sky overwhelmed her. She was flying, anchored to earth only by a long tether of nylon rope.

"Hello, Mark," she said against the wind. "Are you watching?"

7

Brandon became April's constant companion. Whenever he wasn't attending classes or working, he either went to her house or took her to do something. His father was working almost round the clock, taking trips that stretched for days at a time, which Brandon decided was the best thing for both of them. It kept them from fighting. Besides, Brandon liked being with April. He liked her parents too. They catered to her, but she seemed unaffected by their lavish indulgences. The contrast between Brandon's home life and hers was startling to him. Even when his mother had been alive his home life had never been like April's. And even though his father made plenty of money, his home had never had the warmth and togetherness of the one her parents rented on St. Croix.

He made good on his promise to take her sailing one Sunday afternoon toward the end of May. He borrowed a two-person sailboat from a friend and, hitching it to a trailer, drove with April to the far west end of the island, where powder-white beaches surrounded a boat launch. Once they were out on the water, he gave her the tiller.

"What am I supposed to do?" she squealed, gripping the lever that was attached to the rudder that steered the boat.

"Just keep her headed into the wind. If the sail starts to flap or go slack, move the tiller and chase the wind."

Chase the wind. April had never experienced such sheer exhilaration as she did in the sailboat. Even parasailing didn't compare. She was intoxicated by the rise and fall of the bow as it sliced through the water, the sound of the sail filling with wind, and the salty spray of the water wetting her face. She wondered if Mark would have loved it too. He'd been fascinated with fast cars, but she'd never cared much for the smell of exhaust and the noise of roaring engines. The scent of the sea and the sound of the breeze were much more to her liking.

She watched Brandon covertly. His sun-streaked brown hair was windblown and his skin glowed with a golden tan. He wore a bright red tank top and swimming trunks that showed off his muscular arms and legs. She realized with a start that she was attracted to him and that she cared for him. After Mark, she'd never thought she would care for another guy. And, she reminded herself, with her medical history, she shouldn't be thinking about such things. It wasn't fair to Brandon.

"Bring her about!" Brandon shouted, snapping April back to the present.

April turned the tiller until the sail went slack. The boat floundered.

"Watch out for the boom when it comes around."

The bottom arm of the mainsail slowly swung around as the sail filled again, and as the sail changed directions, so did the boat.

"You're very good at this," Brandon said, moving to sit beside her near the tiller. "You sure you've never sailed before?"

She shook her head. "But you can bet I'll

do it again. Tell me about your boat—the one in dry dock."

"It's a thirty-two-footer with beautiful teak decks. It can sleep four and has a galley—that's a kitchen—and it was built in Denmark."

"Who taught you how to sail?"

A faraway look crept into his blue eyes. "It was my mother's boat, really. She's the one who taught me how to sail."

He told her nothing else, but she sensed his sadness at being reminded of his mother. She was sorry she'd brought it up. "Well, thanks for bringing me today and for taking the time to teach me. It's wonderful fun."

"Maybe your father could get you a small boat. There's got to be water up where you live."

Now it was April's turn to back away emotionally. She knew that her time on St. Croix was limited. That sooner or later she'd have to go home. And at home, she'd have to figure out what to do with the rest of her life. "The water around Long Island can sometimes get cold," she said. "It's not the same as St. Croix."

When Brandon dropped her off late in the

afternoon, he asked, "How about dressing up and going to dinner with me tonight? I'll take you to the Buccaneer. They have a band that plays on Saturday nights. A rock group, not one of those snooze bands."

She hadn't dressed up in a long time and thought it might be fun. In the house, she found a note from her mother that she'd gone grocery shopping and that Kelli had called from Oregon. April looked at her watch, realized that it was not yet noon in Oregon, and hurried to the phone. The sound of her friend's voice brought a lump to her throat.

"I miss you and wanted to hear your voice," Kelli said. "The term's over in three weeks."

Kelli had a whole year of college behind her. April felt a pang of regret that she couldn't say the same for herself. "So will you go home for the summer?"

"Not right away." Kelli sighed. "My folks aren't going to make it, April. Dad was in Seattle last week on business and he came to see me. He said he and Mom were calling it quits."

"Gee, I'm sorry." But April wasn't surprised. She'd known that Kelli's parents had struggled for years to keep their marriage together. "What are you going to do?"

"I'm staying here for the summer term. And I've got a job waiting tables at a coffeehouse in town. I figure I'll take some extra hours and save up spending money. My parents are selling the house. Mom's going to stay in New York, but Dad's relocating to Denver. And you're all the way in St. Croix. I feel like a homeless person."

April heard a catch in Kelli's voice, and her heart went out to her friend. "You could come here," she suggested.

"I can't. I have to go to New York after the summer term to see Mom. I hate missing St. Croix, but right now I don't see it happening any other way. When will you go home?"

"I'm supposed to go for another checkup and battery of CAT scans in August, so I guess that's when we'll leave here for good."

"How are you feeling?"

"Sometimes I get light-headed, but no headaches." The debilitating headaches the year before had been her warning that her childhood brain tumor had resumed growing.

"Maybe you should get your checkup sooner."

"I'm sick of doctors. I don't want to see another one ever again."

"Yes, but—"

"But nothing. Don't worry about me. I'm doing fine and I'm having a good time. I go to the beach every day."

"Do you think you'll go back to NYU in the fall?" April had been attending New York University when she and Mark had decided to get married.

"Probably . . . maybe . . . I don't know, Kelli, I just don't know what I want to do."

"How about the rest of you? Are you feeling better about Mark?"

"I'll always miss Mark. But I've met someone here, Brandon Benedict. He's been pretty nice to me and it's helped me sort out what happened to Mark and me."

"Why, that's awesome!" Kelli's delight crackled through the phone line. "Now I really feel bad about not coming. What's he like?"

April told Kelli as much as she could about Brandon. "I know he's got some family problems, but I understand how it feels to lose someone you love. I mean, to have his mother die when he was a high-school senior was hard for him."

"Sounds as if you're good for each other."

"I don't know about that, but I do know I like being with him."

"April, I have to go. I have an exam in a half hour. Just promise me you'll get home in August, same as me. I really want to see you."

"It's a deal." The lump rose again in her throat. "I miss you, Kelli."

"I miss you too."

April hung up and stared out to sea. New York and her other life seemed far away and almost dreamlike. Sometimes she could hardly recall what her house looked like. Or the faces of her old friends. Or even Mark. Quickly she went to her dresser and seized the framed photo of him. She studied Mark's face, memorizing every detail until her heart stopped thudding. *I won't forget you. I won't!* She hugged the photo to herself until the cool glass warmed from the heat of her body.

"Wow. You look beautiful." Admiration danced in Brandon's eyes. He sat across from her at a small table on the restaurant's veranda, out under the stars.

She smiled her thanks. Brandon looked good to her too. He wore a suit, the first she'd ever seen him in, and she liked the effect. "Nice place," she told him.

"Nice company," he returned, giving her a look that made her heartbeat quicken. "We had a senior dance here last year. I didn't go."

She didn't ask why, and he didn't volunteer. She asked, "Isn't the school year about over?"

"I'm taking exams now."

"What will you do this summer?"

"Work until it's time to go off to school."

"Have you picked a college yet?" She remembered his telling her about being accepted into several colleges in the States.

"No. But that's not what I want to talk about. I want to know how much longer you plan to be on the island."

"Maybe until August."

"Perfect," he said, leaning forward. "Then

we can leave together—you to go home, me
to go off to college."

It didn't seem like a bad idea to her. It
would be fun to spend the summer with
Brandon, and after so many months of unhappiness, she felt in the mood to have some
fun. She was sure her parents wouldn't ob-
ject—

"Hello, son."

The man who stood next to their table interrupted April's train of thought. She saw
Brandon stiffen and his expression harden.
"Hi, Dad." Brandon squirmed uncomfort-
ably.

"Aren't you going to introduce us?" Brandon's father stared down at April.

She saw Brandon's likeness in his face, but
his coloring was darker. Saving Brandon the
chore, she said, "Hi. I'm April Lancaster."

Brandon's father smiled. "I suspected
there was someone special taking up Brandon's spare time. Since you're having dinner,
would you care to join us?" He gestured
toward a table across the room, and a deeply
tanned, pretty, dark-haired woman dressed in
white waved. "If I'd known you were coming
here—"

"No thanks." Brandon cut off his father. "We were just leaving." He stood, and his napkin flopped onto the floor.

April questioned him with her eyes. They hadn't even ordered. What was so terrible about joining his father for dinner?

"Come on, April." Brandon held out his hand, and she took it hesitantly and stood.

She saw color in his father's cheeks and realized he'd been stung by Brandon's rudeness. "Um—nice to meet you," she called as Brandon hustled her out of the dining room.

Outside, in the humid tropical night, he skidded to a stop and took a couple of deep breaths. She saw that he was trembling. "What's going on?"

"I didn't expect my father to pop in on us."

"He just said hello," she said, defending him. "Was it seeing him with another woman? I mean, if your mother's been dead for more than a year—"

"And it's his fault!" Brandon blurted out hotly. "She's dead and it's all his fault."

8

Shocked by Brandon's accusation, April gasped. "What are you talking about?" He'd never openly discussed his mother's death with her, nor had she asked him for details.

"Let's walk," Brandon said. "Would you mind?"

"I don't mind."

He led her through well-lit paths to the garden area, where the accent lighting was noticeably dimmer and stars peeked through palm branches. He found an empty bench and sat, his forearms resting on his thighs, his head bowed. "I'm sorry," Brandon said, sounding subdued. "I didn't mean to sound off back there."

Sitting beside him, she asked, "Well, now that you have, tell me what you meant. How is your father responsible for your mother's death?"

"I've never told you how my mother died."

"No, you haven't." She imagined a car wreck with Brandon's father driving.

"My mother committed suicide."

Just the sound of the word made her stomach lurch. *Suicide.* It sounded violent, irrevocable. And she couldn't imagine anyone choosing to die. "How?"

"She took the sailboat out one afternoon. She wrote a note to us, swallowed some pills, and died. The coast guard found the boat drifting and went on board and found her. She loved that boat. She turned it into her coffin."

And April knew that Brandon had loved the boat too. He'd learned to sail on it, and now it held bad memories. "Is that why it's in dry dock?"

"Yeah. Dad hauled it out of the water after Mom's funeral and it hasn't been wet since."

"Would you want to be on it again?"

"Yes." His answer was so soft, she had to lean forward to hear it. "It was the only place I remember her being happy. We spent a lot of time on it together when I was a kid. We sailed for hours and . . . and . . . I miss it."

"Maybe if you talk to your father—"

"Forget it. He didn't care when Mom was alive. He doesn't care now."

"Are you sure?" She remembered when she'd thought her parents were against her union with Mark and how she had attempted to plan her wedding on her own. She'd needed her mother, but believed that her mother was ignoring her by staying uninvolved. It hadn't been true, but the rift between them had turned into a gulf in no time. "I mean, how do you know?"

"I know because he's never home. His business"—he fairly spat the word—"is much more important to him than we ever were. She was so lonely. And it got worse and worse as I grew up."

"Maybe you just noticed it more and more."

He snapped his head up to glare at her. "I know how things were at the house. My mother didn't have any friends except for my father, and he ignored her. She started drinking just to get his attention, she told me. But that didn't work either. Suicide became her only way to get noticed." Brandon shook his head. "It was his fault, all right. He could have stopped her if he'd only paid attention to her. If he'd only seen how much she was hurting."

April didn't agree with his reasoning. "But don't you think she had a choice, Brandon? Don't you think she could have gotten help if she'd really wanted it?"

"My mom wasn't like that. She didn't want the whole world to know her problems. No, my father should have been more sensitive to her."

"*You* were sensitive to her, and that didn't stop her," April said before she realized how her words would hurt him.

He pulled back in horror. "Don't you think I tried? I wanted to help; I skipped school some days when she was really low just to keep her company. But other days I got caught up in the things I wanted to do—seeing my friends, dating, having fun. In the end, I let her down too."

"But you were a kid. You *should* have been busy with those things."

He grunted his disapproval at her willingness to let him off the hook.

April's heart went out to him. He was tortured by thoughts and feelings that didn't seem valid to her. She'd talked to Mark enough to know that some things people can change and some things they can never change, and that it did no good to beat yourself up over the things you couldn't control. "It's like hating yourself because you have blue eyes," he'd told her during one of their discussions about their illnesses. "I was hurt by the way people treated me because I had CF, but while I couldn't control their feelings, I could control mine. I learned to live with it and to be friends with the kids who did overlook my disease."

She knew illness wasn't an easy burden to carry. She hadn't wanted to be pitied or to be made to feel like a freak by kids she knew, but when the truth had come out about her tumor, her real friends stuck by her. Others, like her onetime boyfriend Chris Albright, had dropped her. *His loss.* She said, "Brandon, don't blame yourself. And don't blame your father."

He jumped to his feet. "I didn't expect you to take his side."

"I'm not taking anybody's side," she insisted, grabbing hold of his hand. "Except for you, I never knew anybody in your family. How can I take sides? I'm just wondering if either you or your father could have stopped your mother no matter what you did. She made the choice to die, Brandon. She took the pills all by herself."

"He should have figured out what she planned to do," he insisted stubbornly. "He was *married* to her."

"Being married can't stop something bad from happening to a person, no matter how hard you try."

"How can you understand? I'm sorry I told you. Just forget it."

April could have told him plenty. She could have told him she was no stranger to the pain of feeling helpless and powerless. She could have told him about her brain tumor. But he didn't need the added shock right now, and she didn't need to become too embroiled in a relationship with him. She wanted to be around him as long as they could be friends and have fun. At the end of the summer, they would go their separate ways. "You're right," she told him quietly. "I don't understand, but please don't be sorry we talked about it. I'm not. It helps me to understand you better. And you're the one I care about. I'll never bring it up again, if that's what you want."

He stared at her. "I—I didn't mean to yell at you. I know you were just trying to help." He dropped beside her on the bench and took her shoulders in his hands. "I've never met anybody like you, April. It's like you can sometimes see inside me, and that makes me scared because I'm afraid you'll see all this bad stuff and hate me."

"We all have bad stuff inside us. I could never hate you, Brandon."

"I'm not used to talking about . . . about what happened to my mother. I miss her."

"I miss Mark."

His eyes, only inches from her face, looked moist. "He was very lucky to have you to love him." She felt her heart thudding and heard her pulse roaring in her ears. "I know I could never take his place, and I'm not trying to, but April, I really like you. I . . . would . . . like . . . to kiss you."

Her mouth went dry and she wanted to tell him, *"No, don't,"* but couldn't force her lips to say the words. She had kissed no one except Mark in more than a year, but suddenly, with all her heart, she wanted to kiss Brandon. She raised her chin in acceptance. He pulled her closer and tenderly kissed her parted lips.

So, this is what it feels like to fall in love, Brandon thought as he sat on the sofa in the great room of his house, mindlessly flipping through TV channels with a remote control. His best friend, Kenny, had tried to describe the emotion when Kenny had fallen for his latest girl. "It's a rocket ride, man. You feel like Superman and you want to walk on the clouds."

Well, Brandon agreed. Ever since the night before with April, he'd wanted to fly. She was everything he'd ever dreamed about having in a girlfriend—beauty, brains, sensitivity. He loved her, but he was afraid to tell her. She was still entangled with the memory of her dead fiancé, and Brandon wasn't certain how to untie her from her past love and get her to see him as a new one. His attraction, his attachment to her, had been happening for months, but it had all come to a head when he'd opened his heart concerning his mother. A pang shot through him as he realized the two of them would never meet.

His father's bedroom door opened, and his dad wandered sleepily down the hall. He stopped when he saw Brandon. "I didn't know if you'd be home."

Brandon flipped off the TV and looked at his father. "I have exams next week."

"You, um, doing okay with them?"

"If you're asking if I'm going to pass this year, the answer's yes."

His father went into the kitchen area that adjoined the great room. "You want some coffee?"

"I've had some, but there's more in the pot."

His father sat down at the breakfast bar that separated the two rooms and sipped his coffee. "It's good. Thanks for making it."

Brandon shrugged. Suddenly a thought

occurred to him as he remembered the pretty woman having dinner with his father last night. He stiffened and glanced down the hall toward his father's bedroom. "You are alone, aren't you?"

"I'm alone. Elaine's a nice woman and I'm sorry you and your girl didn't join us for dinner. Can you tell me a little about April?"

Brandon told his father about their meeting, her family, the plans the two of them had made for the summer. "I want to show her a great time before she leaves in August."

His father set down his cup. "She's a beautiful girl, son. And you looked as if you were having a good time with her. That's good. You should be having a good time. Maybe I could take the two of you to lunch sometime."

The offer surprised Brandon because the two of them rarely did things together, mostly because Brandon hadn't wanted to be around his father. "Maybe," he said.

"No one can show April a better time than you. You know this island like the back of your hand." His father sounded downright buoyant.

"I took her sailing. She liked that."

A heartbeat of silence; then his father said, "Sailing's a lot of fun, and you're a good sailor."

But not fun for us, Brandon thought. He stood. "Well, maybe I'd better go cram for today's test. Graduation ceremony is next Saturday," he added. "In case you want to come."

"Of course I want to come. You're my son and graduation is a big day. We'll do something afterward—lunch at the club. Oh, and be thinking about what you want as a gift. If there's anything special. If not, you'll have to take potluck."

I want my mother back. "I'll let you know." Brandon left the room without saying another word.

9

Brandon invited April and her parents to his graduation ceremony, and his father extended an invitation to all of them for dinner at the yacht club. Although the graduating class was small, the ceremony in the school's auditorium was well attended. Brandon ripped off his cap and gown as soon as his father finished taking pictures outside in front of the school seal. "This thing is suffocating me," he grumbled.

"I hated mine too," April assured him. "My friend Kelli said we looked as if we were wearing waffles on our heads."

She looked gorgeous to him, dressed in a summery cotton dress. Her long coppery hair caught the sun and shimmered. He saw her take several pills at the water fountain and asked, "You all right?"

"Fine. Just a slight headache. It'll pass."

At the yacht club, Brandon's father had reserved a table overlooking the sparkling blue waters of the ocean, where sailboats glided in a stiff westerly breeze. Brandon's father and April's parents seemed to have plenty to talk about, which gave Brandon the opportunity to concentrate on April. He told her, "I know my summer work schedule at the golf course—mornings from six until noon. I cut back on my hours—no weekends. That way I'll have every afternoon and evening free. I want to spend as much time as I can with you."

She rubbed her temples. "You didn't have to do that."

"Why not? You do want to do stuff together, don't you? You haven't changed your mind?"

"What about your other friends? Don't you want to be with them? I shouldn't hog all your free time."

"I was sort of a loner this year, April, and so I don't fit in too good anymore. Most of my friends are going away, and my friend

Kenny is stuck on his girlfriend still, so I wouldn't see much of him anyway."

"This might be your last chance to be with your friends. Once high school is over, everyone goes their separate ways."

"I should care? Until I leave for the States in August, I want to spend all my time with you." Suddenly embarrassed, he added, "I mean, that is, if you want to spend the time with me."

A slow smile lit her face. "Of course I do. It'll be a super summer. But it's okay if you change your mind at any time and want to include others in your life."

He nodded but knew that she was the only person in the world he wanted to be with. There was no one else. And perhaps there never would be anyone as special as April in his life again.

The room was spinning. April lay on her bed clutching the sheets, feeling as if she were caught in a whirlwind. *Stop! Stop!* Her vertigo had come on gradually over the past few weeks, sometimes making her feel as if she were aboard the pitching hull of a sailboat, sometimes as if she were being sucked into a

whirlpool. She knew better than to try and
stand; she'd fall over and the thud would
bring her mother running, and the questions
would start: "How long have you been having dizzy spells?" "Do you have headaches
too?" "Why didn't you tell us?" "We're calling your doctor." "We're going back to New
York immediately!"

April knew what would happen if they
found out she was experiencing problems,
and she didn't want to leave. She loved it
here. She was happy. She didn't want to
break her promises to Brandon. The loss of
his mother had been devastating. How could
she add to his unhappiness? The two of them
were supposed to go sailing today. Brandon
had told her, "I'll pack a picnic lunch and
take you to a special little island where we can
snorkel. You'll love it."

Her forehead broke into a sweat, and she
felt nauseated. She swallowed a couple of
pills, took deep breaths, and prayed for the
vertigo to pass. She didn't want to think
about what might be causing it. Perhaps it
was only the start of an inner-ear infection.
Or maybe she was anemic again. Iron defi-

ciency was common in girls her age. She'd been treated for it while she was still in high school. It couldn't be something horrible . . . like the tumor . . . it couldn't be. She wanted more time.

Slowly the room stopped spinning, and she sat up shakily. As soon as she ate breakfast, she'd feel better. She wobbled to her private bathroom, where she showered and changed into a bathing suit. By the time she got to the breakfast table, she felt better. Her father was off playing golf, and her mother was reading the morning mail.

"A letter from Caroline," her mother said as April poured herself a glass of orange juice. "She says the things I shipped last month have really sold well in the store. She wants me to send more."

"Can you?"

"Brandon's father told me about an auction next week at one of the old sugar plantations on the west end of the island. I think I'll go. Why don't you come with me?"

April had often attended auctions with her mother and found them exciting, with people bidding against one another for estate furniture—the once-prized belongings of generations past. And driving from one end of the island to the other took little time. But April didn't want to commit to such a long day. What if she started feeling sick? "I've promised Brandon we'd do some things together."

"It's only one day. And you spend most of your free time with him as it is."

"Mom—please don't pressure me."

"I'm not pressuring you." Her mother set down Caroline's letter. "Honey, I'm glad you've got a friend like Brandon; he's a nice young man. I just think it would be nice for us to do something special together."

"I'll think about it," April hedged.

"Pity about his mother." April had told her parents about Mrs. Benedict's suicide.

"He doesn't talk about it much. I think he feels as if there was something he should have done to stop her."

"I knew a woman once whose mother committed suicide, and she really had a hard time getting over it. If a person ever really does get over such a thing. That's one of the things that's so pitiful about it. The victim's family often feels somehow responsible, although psychiatrists say that's not true."

"That's what I told him. But he's mad at his father, as if *he* might have somehow stopped her."

"My friend was angry for a long time too. Truth was, she was angry at her mother for killing herself, but she couldn't tell her how she felt. She couldn't do anything except suffer mentally."

April understood. She saw how much Brandon was suffering over his mother's death. Even she felt angry at Brandon's mother for making him hurt so badly. She hoped he would be able to find some path out of his pain and make peace with his father. There was nothing she could do to help him. Worst of all, she was only going to go away from him too.

Brandon set sail with April to a tiny, isolated island called a cay, several nautical miles from St. Croix. "These cays are all over the place," he told her. "They're made up of sand and coral rock, and I'll bet I've explored every one of them. Mom and I used to anchor off-

shore and swim in to search for shells." He'd
borrowed a bigger boat than the first one
he'd taught April to sail. She took the tiller
under his direction, turning the mainsail into
the stiff breeze, tacking and coming about
until the boat approached the white-sand cay
he'd chosen for their picnic.

He jumped off into waist-high water and
guided the boat ashore, then jammed the
keel, the part of the boat that balanced it underwater, into the soft sand bottom. The sun
seared through the shallow depths. She could
see every ripple in the sand below. A crab
scurried out of the way.

April helped Brandon carry their gear
ashore. He pitched a small dome-shaped tent
to shield them from the brutal heat of the
sun. They spread out large towels and set
down a cooler and a picnic basket. Brandon
raised side flaps to catch the tropical breeze.
"This is great," she told him, stretching out
on her stomach so that she could gaze at the
water lapping the shoreline and the boat.

"Well, don't get comfortable yet. We're
going snorkeling." From a mesh bag he
dragged out two sets of flippers, two face
masks, and two bright orange snorkel tubes.

She held up the flippers. "You must be kidding. I'll look like a giant frog."

"With red hair," he joked. "Don't scare the fish." He pulled out a large bottle of sunscreen.

"I've already put some on me."

"You'll need more."

She turned her back and lifted her mass of hair, quickly twisting it into a knot and fastening it with a scrunchie. He drizzled the cool lotion on her warm skin, making her shiver involuntarily. His big hands smoothed it along her back and down her arms. He didn't hurry.

"Now what?" she asked, not meeting his gaze, her flesh tingling from his touch.

"Now we hit the water."

She followed him to the water's edge, where she put on the flippers and the mask. After a few minutes of instruction, he led her out deeper and helped her to float facedown. Below the surface, she clearly saw the white-sand bottom and Brandon's flippered feet. He towed her farther out to a coral reef shelf, and the undersea world changed dramatically. Fish, in shades of yellow, green, and even purple and silver, darted through a forest of living vivid-red coral. Starfish clustered around coral branches, their arms hugging the surfaces for dear life.

Once she got the hang of it, April easily sucked air through her snorkeling tube. Brandon never let go of her hand, and together they floated like voyagers from another planet. He tapped her shoulder and pointed to their left. She stared, awed, as a giant manta ray swam past, flapping its wings like a quiet bird of prey, its undersides flashing white in the blue water. Shafts of sunlight streamed downward, lighting beds of coral like spotlights that faded as the coral shelf dropped off and the ocean grew deeper, darker.

A curious parrot fish swam up to her mask, its bright blue lips making silent statements no human could understand. Startled, she flapped an arm, and the fish zipped away to the safety of the reef below. Brandon tapped her shoulder again, and she turned in time to spot a sea turtle, large as a rock but as buoyant in the water as Styrofoam, swimming downward. The world beneath the sea captivated April, and when Brandon pointed toward the shore, she didn't want to go.

"I loved it!" she squealed once they were back under the tent. "I had no idea it was so beautiful down there."

"Scuba diving's even more fun. But you need a tank and some lessons first," he said with a laugh. Bringing her pleasure, seeing her happy, made his heart swell. The girls who'd grown up on St. Croix were unimpressed by such sights, but showing it to April was like seeing it for the first time himself.

"Will you take me scuba diving?"

He laughed at her childlike enthusiasm. "I told you, this is your summer to do anything you want—" He stopped in midsentence. Suddenly April had lain back on the towel, her eyes squeezed shut, her face pale and pinched. Beads of sweat popped out on her forehead. The towel was wadded in her fists, as if she were trying to hold herself in place on the ground. "April! What's wrong? What's happening to you?"

10

Fear ripped through Brandon.

"Dizzy . . . ," April mumbled. "Very dizzy."

He tore the lid off the cooler, grabbed a handful of ice, and pressed it to her temples and throat. "Sit up. Maybe you're hyperventilating."

He helped her sit, but a wave of nausea made her groan.

"Take deep breaths," he said, pressing more ice against the back of her neck.

Nothing was helping. April couldn't stop the world from spinning. She sagged, folded against him, clung for dear life. He stroked her hair, held her in his lap, soothed her skin with a damp towel. "Breathing through your mouth for so long probably made you dizzy," he said, trying to comfort both of them.

With all her heart, she wanted to believe him, but she knew it wasn't so. She was sick and experiencing vertigo and there was only one explanation. "It'll pass," she said weakly, all the while praying, *Please make it go away. Don't let me be sick in front of him.*

"I'm really sorry, April. I wanted today to be fun."

She should have known her medical problem would catch up with her sooner or later. Why, *why* couldn't it have done so later? Tears squeezed from behind her closed eyelids. "It isn't your fault." She knew she should tell him the truth about herself, but all she remembered in the darkness behind her closed eyes was the expression on his face when he'd told her about his mother's suicide. How could she wound him again? Wouldn't it be better to simply let him think she was sick from some other cause? Anything—except the truth? "I—I think I ate some bad fish at supper last night. I wasn't feeling all that great when I got up this morning, but I wanted to come so badly that

I made myself feel better. I guess it's finally caught up with me. So much for the power of positive thinking."

"Let me pack up and get you home," he said. "Lying out here in the heat isn't helping you any."

She agreed, but she didn't want to go. She wanted to stay on this sandy strip of island and be with him. She wanted to feel the warmth of the sun. She wanted to hear the gentle sloshing of the sea against the shoreline. She wanted to remain in paradise. A headache crept up the back of her neck and settled around her head like a vise. The pain turned her skin clammy.

She heard him moving around and concentrated on the sounds he made, trying not to think about the mounting pain of the headache. He took the tent down last, after gently carrying her to the boat. The swaying of the boat caused her to totally lose her equilibrium. She felt like a matchstick tossed on a sea of waves, unable to get her bearings.

"I wish this thing had a motor," he grumbled. "Our boat has a motor. But my father won't take our boat out of dry dock."

Brandon was talking to no one but the

wind. Every time he looked down at the pale, motionless April, his heart lurched. She'd got sick so quickly. He'd been taken completely by surprise. His mother's moods had been mercurial—one minute she was happy, the next depressed—but eventually depression had won her over to its dark ways. That was his only experience with sickness, and even though her sickness had been in her mind, it had affected her physically.

He recalled days when she couldn't pull herself out of bed. He recalled nights when she drank and walked the floors, crying inconsolably. He'd felt helpless. And he felt helpless now. April's skin looked pale as paste, and she'd put a damp towel over her eyes. He didn't want anything to happen to her. He loved her. Of course, he couldn't tell her because he doubted she would believe him. And she loved the mysterious Mark. How did a guy compete with a dead person?

Fortunately, a stiff breeze allowed Brandon to make good time, and as soon as he arrived at the Buccaneer, he tossed his friend Billy the lines and shouted that he'd be back later for the gear. He got April into his car and drove as fast as he dared to her house.

He screeched into her driveway, leaped out, and ran to the front door. When her mother opened the door, he told her that April was sick.

Janice's eyes went wide, and the color left her face. "Help me get her into her room."

Again, Brandon carried her. Janice had thrown back the covers, and he laid April on the bed and stepped aside while her mother hovered over her. "Should you call a doctor?" Brandon asked. "You could call the one my mother—we use." He corrected himself.

"I'll call her doctor back home," Janice said, grabbing the phone.

"All the way in New York? We have doctors here."

"It's all right. He knows April."

"Whatever." He surveyed the room, April's room, filled with signs of April's life. Perfume bottles on the dresser. Bathing suits, a whole collection, piled in a heap near the closet door. A framed photo on her bedside table of a grinning guy in an auto racing uniform. *Mark.* He knew it instinctively. A knot formed in his stomach, seeing the image of his dead rival. So this was the guy she'd planned to marry. Brandon had wondered about him, about why she'd fallen in love with someone with cystic fibrosis. Why would she consider devoting herself to caring for a sick person? What magic power had Mark held over her?

Brandon heard April's mother talking softly into the phone, using words he didn't understand and phrases he couldn't quite catch.

She turned toward him. "Brandon, will you do me a favor? My husband is playing golf at the country club today. Would you go find him and tell him what's happened?"

"Sure." Brandon was glad to have something to do. "She will be all right, won't she? I mean, maybe you should take her to the emergency room. Maybe it's more than eating bad fish. Maybe it's food poisoning."

"Bad fish? Is that what she told you?"

"Yes."

Janice nodded. "As soon as her father gets here, we'll check it out."

"I'm on my way." Brandon strode to the door.

"Thank you," April's mother called. "Thank you for taking care of her."

He glanced back to see that her face was

still pale but her expression was calm, almost serene. And incredibly sad. It startled him, but he didn't have time to think about it. Brandon jumped into his car and drove like a madman toward the country club golf course.

"Why didn't you say something, April? Why didn't you tell us what was going on?" The tremor in her father's voice betrayed his attempt to be stern with her.

"I didn't say anything because I knew how you'd panic." She felt fuzzy, still floating from the effects of the shot of morphine the doctor at the hospital had given her. The headache had subsided for now.

"Panic?" her mother said. "You pass out from pain and you think we might panic? Over such a small, ordinary thing like that?"

"Don't be sarcastic, Mom. I'm sorry I didn't say something to you, but I just didn't want everything to end. I knew what was happening, but I didn't want to admit it."

Her father stroked her arm. "We don't know for sure what's happening. We have an appointment to see Dr. Sorenson in New York the day after tomorrow."

"I don't want to go home."

"He wants to run tests."

"I'm sick of tests. We all know what the tests are going to tell him. They're going to say that the tumor's growing again. And he's going to say the same thing he told us last year. There's nothing else medical science can do for me!" Her voice had risen, and in spite of the calming effects of the morphine, she began to cry.

Her mother scooped her into her arms, rocked her, and cooed, "Oh, baby. Oh, my sweet little girl."

"I'm not giving up," her father insisted. "You're our daughter, April. You mean everything to us. I won't let them tell us there's nothing else that they can do. I don't believe it."

April wept silently into her mother's shoulder, missing Mark, then Brandon. Life was being sucked away from her, snatched like a purse stolen by a thief. She'd known her prognosis all along. No one had ever hidden the truth from her. Maybe it would have been better if they had hidden it. The knowledge was overwhelming. *Goodbye to paradise*.

"I'm going to make arrangements now,"

her father said. "We'll pack what we need. And what we don't take we can get at home. We have a house full of stuff on Long Island."

"Will we come back?" April's voice sounded dull and thick.

"Probably not."

She winced as if he'd struck her.

Her mother smoothed her hair. "Do you want to call Brandon? Would you like me to call and talk to him?"

"No. I'll call him from New York."

"Are you sure?"

April pictured his face. He would pity her. Or worse, he'd withdraw the way her old boyfriend Chris had when she'd told him about her tumor. Better to go away and call Brandon and tell him over the phone. The miles between them would act as a cushion to soften his reaction. "I'm sure," she said finally. "When he calls later"—as she knew he would—"just tell him I'm resting and that I'll talk to him when I'm able."

"If that's what you want," her mother said in a tone that told April she didn't agree with her plan.

"That's what I want."

The island of St. Croix slipped away under a blanket of clouds below the airplane's window. The water turned into a rippled piece of blue taffeta, and April could scarcely bear to look down at it. Like spoils from an old corsage, a few hand-picked hibiscuses lay on her lap, the red and pink petals' edges wilting, the yellow pollen clinging to her fingers. She felt terrible. The pills the doctor had prescribed made her feel groggy and out of sync, but at least there was no headache. She imagined Brandon coming to the house, knocking on the door, seeing the note. Hastily she'd scribbled: WE HAD TO LEAVE. FAMILY PROBLEMS BACK HOME. I'LL CALL YOU IN A FEW DAYS. Of course, it was all lies. She hoped she'd have the courage to talk to him soon. Tears wet her face as the plane climbed higher and the sea slipped away under more clouds. She closed her eyes and allowed the medication to lull her into a drugged sleep.

Brandon stared at the note, incredulous. April was gone. Just like that. Not even a word of goodbye. She could have called. She could have told him personally or even over the phone. He turned the piece of paper over, hoping for more of an explanation on the back. It was blank.

She could have said, *"See you soon."* Or *"I'll miss you."* But she hadn't. She and her family had sneaked away, leaving him with a hundred unanswered questions. The hibiscus bush next to the porch had been picked clean, all the flowers gone, the leaves shining green in the sun. He knew she'd taken them with her. But he also realized that she'd taken much more than the rich red and pink flowers. She'd also taken his heart.

11

July in New York was just as hot, humid, and sticky as April remembered. In the past, during the sweltering days, her family had taken vacations into the mountains or to Europe. Except for last year, when she'd been with Mark and hadn't wanted to go anywhere he didn't go. The city felt oppressive to her now, teeming with people in a hurry—a shock to her system after the easygoing atmosphere of St. Croix. Even her childhood home seemed uninviting. Her parents had called ahead to have it opened and aired, but musty odors from having been shut up for months still lingered. Her room had been cleaned and fresh linen put on her bed, but she missed looking out at the sea, missed the aroma of tropical flowers and salt-tinged air, and as much as she hated to admit it, she missed Brandon too. In short, she didn't want to be back home.

On Wednesday morning the three of them headed into the city for the hospital and the rounds of testing she didn't want to face. Two days later, as they sat in Dr. Sorenson's office, April felt drained and, like a child in a cruel mazelike game, right back at square one—the place she'd started from more than eighteen months before.

Dr. Sorenson was as pleasant as ever, exactly as she remembered him, but he looked preoccupied, more reserved than in past visits. He placed the MRI films on the light board and drew a circle around the now-familiar dense glob pressing against her cerebellum. "It's growing again," he said matter-of-factly, his voice tinged with sadness.

Deep down, it was nothing she hadn't known, but seeing it on the film, hearing him state the obvious, made her suck in her breath. His actual words gave finality to her situation. It closed doors.

"So where do we go from here?" her father asked sharply, after a moment of silence.

Of course, they'd been all through her options before she'd ever left for St. Croix: She had none. The tumor was too aggressive for treatments, too large for gamma knife surgery.

"I wish I had better news for you," Dr. Sorenson said now, picking his words carefully.

"Then this is it, isn't it?" April asked boldly, suddenly wanting to get everything settled once and for all. "There's really nothing else you can do for me, is there?" Tears stung her eyes, but she refused to let them out.

"You've had two rounds of radiation—the maximum—and chemotherapy won't touch this type of tumor. I'm sorry, April."

"Her mother and I won't accept that." Her father struck his fist on the edge of the doctor's desk. "I have money. There are other doctors. Other hospitals."

"Your daughter's prognosis won't change. You can spend thousands, hundreds of thousands; it won't make a difference."

"Experimental drugs," her father shouted. *"Something."*

April recoiled. She didn't want to be somebody's lab experiment.

"If there was anything on the medical horizon to help your daughter, I would have suggested it. Certainly there are quacks in the world, Mr. Lancaster. There are many people who promise cures but can't deliver them. Many charlatans who'll take your money, make April suffer, but not cure her."

"So you're saying we just have to abandon hope? We won't, sir. We can't."

"Oh, Hugh . . . ," April's mother cried. "Do something. Please."

April stood. The last time the doctor had tried to close the door on her hope she'd shouted at him too, and then had run from his office, refusing to listen to any more grim news. And she'd gone on to have a few wonderful months with Mark, followed by spring and most of the summer in St. Croix. This time, she was resigned. "Please stop shouting." Her knees trembled, but she stood her ground and stared at her distraught parents. Unbelievably, a calm settled on her. "It won't help, Daddy. It won't change things. The doctor's out of miracles."

She sat on her mother's lap like a child and nestled her head against her shoulder, reached for her father's hand, and pulled him closer into the circle.

"Oh, baby," her mother wept.

"Tell us, Dr. Sorenson. Tell us what to expect." April was dry-eyed now.

The doctor cleared his throat. "I'll be increasing your steroid medication to keep down the swelling of your brain as the tumor advances."

She winced. Even though the pills had helped the headaches in the past, she'd hated the side effects: weight gain, a puffy moon-shaped face, and swollen hands and feet. The treatment had deepened her voice and made hair grow in usually hairless places on her body. "And then? Please tell me everything."

"You'll have memory lapses, equilibrium problems, trouble with speech and probably sight and hearing. Eventually you'll be bedridden. You'll slip into a coma. Your lungs will fill with fluid, and you'll stop breathing."

The progression sounded logical to her. Her body would slowly shut down as the tumor choked out her life. "Will I have to be in the hospital?"

"No, not if you don't want to be. Hospice

is a wonderful group that helps families keep
their loved ones at home . . . until the end.
You can have a nurse, a hospice member, anyone you want with you."

"I'd like that. I'd like to die at home."

"Except for headaches, which will pass in
time, you won't be in pain. That's a unique
feature of the brain. It has no nerve endings.
That's why we can perform complicated sur-
geries on it with nothing more than a local
anesthetic. Patients can be wide awake
through several types of brain surgery, even
talk to the surgeon and give reports on what
they are feeling."

Cold comfort, April thought. She said, "So,
I'll just go to sleep and not wake up?"

"Yes, that's pretty much how it will be."

It was impossible for her to imagine non-
existence, to think of herself not of this
world. She hugged her mother tightly and
squeezed her father's hand. "I want you with
me the whole time."

"We'll be with you, baby," her mother
whispered. "You know we will."

April closed her eyes, shutting out all but
the sound of her own breathing.

———

Later, April told them she didn't want to talk about it. She wanted to concentrate on what was happening in the here and now, not in the future. But when she was alone, she steeped her senses in touching, tasting, seeing. She walked in the yard, fingered flower petals, sniffed the roses, all the while mourning the loss of them. Once, she held her breath for as long as she could, but gave up and gasped for air just as she started to feel light-headed. Would she do the same thing when she was in a coma? She wished she'd spent more time talking to Mark about dying, about giving up and letting go.

And she thought about Brandon too. She wondered if he hated her for running off without a word. She thought about calling him but wondered what she would say to him. It was as if she were two people: the girl in New York who was dying, and the girl in St. Croix who was carefree and happy and having a wonderful time. How could she merge the two? How could she expect Brandon to understand? She'd been unfair.

She wondered too how his mother could have tossed away her life. The pain her suicide had caused Brandon was immeasurable.

Hadn't she considered what it might do to him? April knew that if she could do anything to hold on to her life, she would. It made no sense to her that someone would throw away what she so desperately wanted.

The hospice people came out to the house to visit, to talk. They were kind people, understanding, with their own losses behind them. But April realized they were more for her parents' benefit than hers. Her parents would be the ones left behind while she would go . . . where? She'd always believed in heaven, had been taught about it in Sunday school. She tried to remember what she'd been told but could only recall that heaven was a place of great beauty where there would be no more sadness or sorrow.

But thoughts of eternal peace and perfect happiness brought her little comfort. There were still so many things she wanted on this side of heaven. She had wanted a career and to get married, maybe to have children. Until now, she'd given no thought to growing old, but suddenly it didn't seem like such a bad thing to do. What would she have looked like? Would her hair color have faded? Would her complexion have wrinkled?

"The trouble," she told herself one morning as she studied her face in the mirror, "is that you have too much time to think." She needed to talk to someone, be with someone other than her parents. Kelli wouldn't be home for another few weeks. April needed someone now. Which was how she ended up calling Mark's mother and making plans to visit her. Yet as she climbed up the steps of the old brownstone on a hot, muggy morning, she felt it might have been a mistake. The pain of the happy memories she'd shared with Mark at his parents' home engulfed her. She almost turned and skittered away, but the door was flung open and Mark's mother, Rosa, threw her arms around April and dragged her into the cool quiet of the foyer.

"Praise be!" Rosa said. "How good to see you, April. When did you get home? How was your trip? You look wonderful! So tan and beautiful." She held April at arm's length, stroking her with her gaze.

To April, Rosa was ever pretty, with lively eyes and black hair sprinkled with gray. She looked so much like Mark, it brought a lump to April's throat. April gave a brief accounting of her time, leaving out her reason for returning to New York.

Rosa herded her into the kitchen, where a giant pot of simmering soup filled the room with its tomato aroma. Rosa sat April down at the table and proceeded to ladle up a bowl of soup. Never mind that April wasn't hungry. "Tell me everything," Rosa insisted, sitting with her at the table. "Did I say that we've missed you? Thank you for the postcards . . . such a beautiful place."

April talked glowingly about St. Croix, not mentioning Brandon, of course, and finished by asking, "How have you all been?"

"Mark's father is well. Still working too hard, but such is a detective's life—there's so much crime out there. And it's good for him to have a job he loves. Marnie and Jill still aren't married, but Marnie's met a nice Italian boy and we have hopes for her."

April smiled, recalling Mark's pretty sisters and their parents' desire to see them married and settled. It didn't seem to matter that both were competent, professional women. To Rosa, marriage and children were the only real-life choice for a woman. "You tell them hello for me."

"Why me? You tell them yourself. Now that you're back, you and your parents can come for dinner."

"We can do that." April felt her mouth getting dry and knew she was having an attack of nerves. There was so much she had to tell Rosa, but how should she begin? "I miss Mark," she confessed. "In St. Croix, I thought about him every day. He would have really liked it there."

Rosa's smile turned wistful. "Not a day goes by that I don't think of him too. I . . . we . . . miss him very much. But I want you to know how much happiness you brought him the last year of his life. I will always love you for that."

"I still have the wedding dress. It's packed away in a huge box in the back of my closet."

"You were beautiful in it. Maybe you can wear it for another."

April dropped her gaze. "I was wondering if you would do me a favor."

"Ask me for anything."

"Come with me to the cemetery. I want to visit Mark's grave."

12

The cemetery stretched green and quiet in the hot sun. Manicured lawns were broken by aboveground mausoleums, statues of saints, and carved stonework and bronze markers with vases. April watched sprinklers spew sprays of water over sections of grass as Rosa drove slowly along the internal roadway toward Mark's grave. The cemetery was more beautiful than April remembered from the day of Mark's burial, but she'd been so numb at the time she'd hardly noticed anything.

"It's over there," Rosa said, stopping the car.

They got out and wound their way through a field of markers until Rosa halted near a weeping willow tree. April stooped down. A marker held Mark's name, his birth and death dates, and the inscription BELOVED SON. AT PEACE FOREVER. Rising over the marker stood a statue of the Virgin Mary, her arms open. A bronze vase held fresh flowers. "I wanted him to always have flowers," Rosa explained. "The groundskeepers put them out once a week for him."

"Do you come often?"

"Maybe once a month. It hasn't been that long, you know."

He had died in the fall. April stared down at the marker, imagining her name etched in the metal. She took a quivering breath. "I'm dying, Rosa." It was the first time she'd ever called Mark's mother by her first name. Always before, she'd addressed her as Mrs. Gianni.

"What?" The woman stepped backward as if she'd been struck.

"The tumor's growing again. There's nothing the doctors can do."

"Oh, April, no. It can't be true."

April looked at her, saw tears swimming in her eyes, and swallowed against the lump of emotion wedged in her own throat. "It's one of the reasons we came home from St. Croix. I started having problems again. We had to get them checked out."

"This isn't right. You don't deserve this."

Mark's family had always known about her brain tumor, but Mark's problems were so overwhelming, Apirl's had taken a backseat. "Mark didn't deserve CF either. We knew that this was a possibility when he and I first met. For a long time, it scared me so much I didn't even want to date him. But he was a hard one to say no to." April smiled, remembering his long pursuit of her and the way he had worn down her resistance. "We loved each other, but sometimes I forgot about the illnesses. I didn't believe either of us would actually . . . you know . . . really die."

"There must be something the doctors can do for you."

"They introduced us to the people at hospice. I don't want to die in the hospital." The memory of Mark's last days haunted her. There had been nothing friendly, nothing comforting about the cool technology of the hospital's machines and antiseptic smells. She wanted her departure from the planet to be different.

Rosa crossed herself. "You mustn't give up."

"I'm not giving up. I'm being realistic. It's better to face the truth than to pretend it isn't happening."

"Is there anything you want me to do for you? Just ask."

"My parents . . . it's hard on them. If you could be here for them . . . you know . . . afterward."

"Absolutely. If they ever want to talk, tell them to call."

Mark's parents knew what it was to lose a child. Funny, April hadn't thought of herself as a child in many years, but she felt like one now. She felt small and frightened. She wanted the bad things to go away. She didn't want to go through what lay ahead.

"And I was thinking . . . do you think I could be buried here? By Mark?" She wasn't Catholic, but all at once it was important to her to think about having a place to belong to, a place for her parents to come and visit.

"I'll talk to my priest. You were planning

on marrying in the church. What can it matter if you want to rest beside your fiancé forever?"

April knelt and ran the palm of her hand across Mark's name. The bronze felt smooth and warm from the sun. Shadows from the willow tree danced across the grass beside her. She too would soon become a shadow, shifting in and out of the sunlight. Her body might be placed below the ground, but her spirit— "You believe Mark's in heaven, don't you?"

"Yes. I believe Mark's with God. The only thing that makes losing him easier is knowing that, and that he isn't in any more pain. The pain he suffered was always the hardest part for me . . . although he rarely complained." She sighed. "Long ago, I resigned myself to knowing that I would never hold a grandchild of his."

Because boys with cystic fibrosis are sterile, April reminded herself. She remembered the night he'd told her he'd never be able to father children. He'd been so afraid she'd leave him. As it was turning out, she'd never give her parents a grandchild either. Her parents' genes, her family tree, ended with her. "Do you think God will tell me why, if I ask him?"

"Why?"

"Why Mark and I had to die. Why we were ever born in the first place."

"I certainly plan to ask him," Rosa said with a shrug. "My priest says God has a reason for everything, but that he doesn't owe us any explanations."

April wondered if once she was dead, she'd understand God's purposes. The meaning of life and God's purposes were too vast a subject to think about now.

She said, "I'm ready to leave now."

"Of course." Rosa began walking to the car.

April followed. In the distance a sprinkler sent water skyward, and in a quirk of the light, a rainbow formed. She watched it shimmer and thought of childhood stories of pots of gold at the rainbow's end. Somehow it seemed fitting, and also a kind of foreshadowing. At the end of the rainbow of her life, the ground would swallow her. And she would lie beside Mark in death, as she had been unable to lie beside him in life.

After hugs and promises to keep in touch, April returned home. Her father insisted on taking April and her mother to a restaurant overlooking Long Island Sound for dinner. They sat in a quiet corner booth with lit candles, watching the sky turn from orange to red to purple with the waning light of the sun.

April stared out at the water, a deep navy blue, so different in color from the intense turquoise of the Caribbean. Lately all things seemed different to her. Music sounded more beautiful, colors appeared more vibrant. Did knowing that she would soon have to leave this world make her time in it more precious? She wasn't sure. She only knew that she felt balanced on the brink between dread and expectation. "I visited Mark's grave today," she told her parents.

They looked startled. "Was that wise?" her father asked.

"I miss him. I wanted to be near him again."

Her mother's lips pressed together. April could tell she didn't approve. "I hope you aren't dwelling on dark thoughts. You should be putting your energy into positive ones.

Doctors don't know everything. Miracles happen."

"Is that what you think will happen for me? A miracle?"

Her mother's face flushed. "I just don't think it's smart to abandon hope."

"I'm not. But I have to know what to hope for. A cure doesn't seem likely. So I have to hope for other things."

"Such as?"

She shrugged. "Courage. The next few months aren't going to be easy. Not for any of us." Her parents said nothing. "Mark's mother said that you should call her. That she knows what you're going through and that she'll be there for you."

April's mother turned her head and jabbed furiously at the napkin in her lap. "I know she means well, but she can't possibly know what I'm feeling. She can't begin to understand how angry I am." Her voice cracked. "You are my only child. Rosa has others."

April blinked, incredulous. Would knowing you had other children make it easier to lose one? "That doesn't make sense."

"And your dying does?"

April's father put out his hand, and April's

mother took it. April watched as their grip on each other tightened and wished she could hang on too. After she was gone, they would still have each other. She was glad of that. "Mom, I don't want to die. I don't want to leave either of you, but I can't help it. Please, don't make me feel as if there's something I should be doing to stop it." Tears welled in her eyes.

"Is that what you think?" Her mother looked stricken. "Do you think I'm holding you responsible because you're dying?"

Her father said, "We know you can't help it, baby. We know it's not your fault."

The incredible sadness of the moment was breaking April's heart. A part of her wished she could save them all from the horrible process that lay ahead for them. But a part of her desperately needed them with her to help make the leaving easier. She felt torn between wanting to spare them and needing them to shield her.

"I'm sorry," her mother whispered. "I had no right to dump my frustrations on you. There's nothing you can do to stop this from happening. There's nothing we can do either. But I feel helpless and powerless. And so very angry. We have all this money, and it counts for nothing when it comes to stopping what's happening. When we wanted a baby, we turned to medicine and it helped us. Now the medical community has abandoned us."

By the time their food arrived, none of them had an appetite. April toyed with her fork, feeling absolutely strung out. She didn't want her last months—maybe only weeks—to be like this, with each of them sad, angry, and locked in a prison of pain. If she allowed it, death would have a double victory over her. And *that* she could not stand. It was hard enough to lose her life. She would not also lose her spirit, her capacity to feel joy and show love. Mark had shown her love up until the very end of his life. His last breath had gone into forming the words "I love you." She couldn't—wouldn't—allow hers to say less. This, then, was her season of goodbye, her farewell to a good life. She vowed to make each and every minute that was left to her count for something.

13

The arrival of April's friend Kelli in mid-August was like a fresh breeze blowing through the stagnant air of April's life. April flung open the front door and they threw themselves into each other's arms. Kelli squealed, "How are you? I've missed you so much!" She dropped her duffel bag on the floor, for they'd already planned that she would spend the night.

"Same here!" April cried. She held Kelli at arm's length. "Wow! You look fabulous! When did you cut your hair?"

"Ages ago. Do you like it?" Kelli spun, showing off her short dark cap of curls. "But look at you! You're absolutely golden brown.

And your hair. I'll bet it's three shades lighter."

"All that sun in St. Croix."

Kelli peered closely at her. "Have you put on weight?"

"Um—I'm back on that headache medicine for a while. You remember how it makes me puff up like a blowfish."

"But why—"

April grabbed Kelli's arm and dragged her up the stairs to her room. "We'll talk about me later. First I want to hear all about you. And college. And your summer job." She scrambled onto the bed and hugged her knees. "So, start talking."

"School's awesome," Kelli said, plopping down across from April, Indian style. "It was scary at first, being so far from home and all, but now I love it. My roommate, Cheryl, is a real athlete—she's on a basketball scholarship—and she lives down in San Francisco, so that's where I crash over major holidays when the school shuts down. She's dragged me hiking and rock climbing and blading—" Kelli ticked off on her fingers. "I've never had so much exercise in my life."

"And classes? You do go to classes, don't
you?"

"I only sleep through the morning ones.
Actually, I like classes. Much better than high
school. Can you believe I'll be a sophomore
in September?"

April didn't need reminding. She too
would have been a second-year college student if only cancer hadn't happened to her.
"And your job? Are you the boss yet?"

"Work is work. But waiting tables at a coffeehouse all summer was kind of fun. I honestly didn't want to quit and come home, but
I had to . . . Mom was pressuring me. She
hasn't seen me since Christmas break, so I
had to make an appearance."

"How is your mom?"

Kelli shrugged, and her bright smile faded.
"She's adjusting to being divorced. She's living in the city now that the house has been
sold, and she's got a job in a florist shop.
She's doing good, but I think she misses her
old friends."

"And your dad?"

"He's into his second childhood out in
Denver. He's dating a girl who's only eight
years older than me. Can you believe it?"

Kelli didn't wait for a response. "What do I care? He's paying my college tuition."

But April could tell that Kelli cared very much. "Any cool guy in your life?" she asked, changing the subject.

"There's Jonathan." Kelli's expression softened. "He's a junior and going for a degree in restaurant management. We worked at the coffeehouse together. He's perfectly wonderful."

"Kelli! Are you *serious* about him?"

"Define *serious*. He makes my knees weak when he looks at me, and when he kisses me the earth moves. Just a crush, I'd say."

April squealed and swatted her friend with a pillow. "You're in love! I know the signs."

"Well . . . maybe just a little. Not as serious as you and Mark were, of course, but I really like him." Kelli's eyes sparkled. "Which leads me to ask about Brandon."

Now it was April's turn to look serious. "I don't think I'm on Brandon's favorite-person list. I, um, sort of ran out on him."

"What do you mean?"

"We left St. Croix in a hurry. I didn't tell him goodbye."

"But why? That's not like you."

"Oh—you know, we waited until the last minute to pack up and then the next thing I knew we were on the plane and on our way."

"You haven't written him? Or called him?"

"I will," April said dismissively. Once again, she wasn't up to confessing the whole truth to Kelli. As long as they could just talk about this and that, she could pretend that she was normal. She could make believe that everything was perfect, and she wouldn't have to tell her best friend that she was dying.

They went for ice cream, and as April drove through the familiar streets she recalled their days of growing up together. Every street corner, every neighborhood, blossomed with memories. The dance studio where they'd taken ballet classes in the third and fourth grades was open and conducting classes, and a group of little girls could be seen doing exercises at the barre through the plate glass window.

Kelli licked her ice-cream cone, not paying much attention to April's meandering tour. "I can't wait to get back to Oregon," she said. "I'd forgotten how muggy summer is around here."

"You're right. It's even cooler in St. Croix than it is here."

"I'm sorry I never got down there to visit you. I would have loved it. Will you go back?"

"Probably not." April regretted not returning. Not merely because she missed the beauty of the island, but also because she would never see Brandon again. All that lay ahead for her now was a downward spiral into sickness. She shifted gears. "How'd you like to run by school?"

"Whatever."

Their former high school, a large redbrick building, had been closed for the summer, but a few of the teachers had returned to prepare for the fall term, so the doors were open. April and Kelli strolled down the empty halls, their footfalls echoing in the quiet. The scent of chalk and white paste sent a wave of nostalgia through April. She'd never thought she would miss the place, but suddenly she did miss it. She'd been an excellent student and had received high honors. Once she'd even dreamed of becoming a TV journalist.

"I wish you could see my campus," Kelli

said, seemingly oblivious to the spell of the building. "It's majorly cool, while this place is so rinky-dink." They'd stopped in front of the trophy case. "Look, there's your name." Kelli pointed to a tall silver award won by the debate team in April's junior year. April's name was etched in the metal.

"That was fun," April said with a wistful smile.

"Immortalized for all time," Kelli said brightly.

April figured that once she was gone, the trophy and photos in the yearbook would be all that remained of her. "I think you should go to the twenty-fifth reunion," she told Kelli.

"Sure. We'll go together." April didn't answer, but headed for the parking lot and the car. "Hey, wait for me," Kelli called, jogging after her. "What's the rush?"

"No hurry. Just thought of somewhere else I'd like to go." April drove slowly and turned down a side street. "Have you been by your old house?"

"Not yet."

"Would you like to?"

"I guess," Kelli said halfheartedly.

The quiet tree-lined street was just as April

remembered it. "The last time I drove down this street was that day last year when you left for college."

"I think I knew then that I wouldn't be back to live here. My folks were barely speaking."

April pulled up to the curb and shut off the engine. The old brick house looked well kept. The shutters and front door had been painted blue, and a stranger's car was in the circular driveway. "I missed you from the second you rolled out of the driveway."

"You were making plans to marry Mark."

"I wish I could have had more time with him."

Kelli stared out at the house for a long time before sighing. "It seems like a million years ago that I lived here."

April heard the emotion in her friend's voice. "I know what you mean. When I got back home, everything seemed out of sync. It was as if I didn't belong here anymore."

"I really *don't* belong here. And I guess my parents' split is for the best. They've been unhappy together for so long. I think they just stayed together because of me. Still, it's weird."

"What's weird?"

"Seeing the house, knowing that someone else lives in it. Knowing I don't have a home anymore—just a college dorm room halfway across the country."

"I didn't mean to make you sad," April said softly.

"I'll get over it. I mean, you were ready to start a new home with Mark last summer. Isn't that the way things are supposed to be? You grow up, move out, get married, and make your own life."

Yes, for some people, April thought. She switched on the engine. "Let's get out of here. It's almost time for supper, and Mom will be miffed if you don't eat with us."

"Has her cooking improved?"

"Not much."

Both girls broke out laughing, and April sped back toward her house, anxious to dispel the gloom that had fallen over them both.

Dinner would have been subdued if not for Kelli's animated chattering. April's father asked questions about college, and Kelli told about her campus, her classes, her aspirations.

"I have to declare a major by the time I'm a junior, and right now I'm leaning toward a degree in public relations. I like working with people, and I'm getting good grades in a couple of advertising classes."

"You'd be good at PR," Hugh told her.

"Maybe April and I can go into business together someday."

April's mother caught April's gaze with a questioning look that asked, *"Haven't you told her?"* and April flashed her a look that said, *"Not yet."*

But once dinner was over and April and Kelli climbed the stairs to April's bedroom, Kelli shut the door firmly behind her and turned to face April. She said, "All right—it's time you told me everything."

"Everything? What do you mean?" April's mouth went dry, and her heart thumped nervously.

"We've talked about everything but you. We've gone a lot of places today and tripped down Memory Lane. I've known you for most of my life, and I know when something is bothering you. Your parents look totally depressed, and I haven't asked you about

your health because I figured out real fast
that you didn't want to talk about it earlier
today. But now I want to know. Please, don't
keep me in the dark any longer. Tell me,
April, what's going on?"

14

April stood in the middle of the room, looked Kelli straight in the face, and told her. She'd thought she would be able to get through the whole story without crying, but as she quietly delivered the news about her impending death, as she watched Kelli's eyes widen and her hand clamp across her mouth to stifle sobs, and saw tears trickle down Kelli's cheeks, April wept with her.

"No! No!" Kelli kept shaking her head.

April closed the distance between them and took her friend in her arms, trying to comfort her. "Don't cry. I hate to see you cry." It struck April as odd that she, the one who was dying, should be comforting the one who was not, but it seemed the right thing to do. Kelli was devastated, and April wanted to help ease her pain. It was as if she were removed from the situation. As if it weren't her they were talking about, but some other person, some mutual friend.

Between sobs, Kelli managed to say, "I knew it was going to be bad news. I knew by the way you were driving around today, visiting all the places where we grew up, that you had something heavy to tell me. Oh, April, I'd give anything if it wasn't this kind of news."

"I wish it was something else too."

"Your doctor . . . he's positive? There isn't any mistake?"

"No mistake." April fumbled for tissue from a box on her vanity and handed a wad to Kelli. "It's been hard to even think about it. Some mornings I wake up and I feel real mellow, and then it hits me: I'm going to die. It sort of spoils the whole day."

Kelli blew her nose and attempted a smile at April's dark humor. "It isn't fair."

"What *is* fair?"

"Well, not *this*!" Kelli sank onto the bed and grabbed April's hand. "That settles it. As long as you're here, I'm not going to leave you. I'm quitting school and moving back home."

"Kelli, you can't drop out of school. I won't let you."

"And I won't let you die without me." Kelli dissolved into fresh tears.

April settled beside her on the bed. "Everybody has to die sometime or another, Kelli. You have to go on with your life."

"I'm putting my life on hold and you can't stop me."

"Look, I don't even know when this might happen to me. You can't sit around in some kind of deathwatch." She made a face. "It's unnatural."

"Says who?"

"Says me. You've planned to go back to Oregon in two weeks, and that's exactly what I want you to do. I—I don't want you to hover over me, waiting for me to keel over."

"That's not what I'll do."

"You won't mean to, but it'll happen. I remember what it was like to watch Mark die. I didn't believe it was happening. I felt helpless because I couldn't stop it. It was a nightmare, and you shouldn't have to go through it."

"And so what am I supposed to do? Sit in Oregon and wait for my phone to ring? Wait for your mother to call and drop the bomb on me?"

"Yes."

Kelli shook her head furiously. "I won't. I won't be three thousand miles away while you . . . while you . . ." She couldn't finish her sentence.

"Everything you've told me about has been about Oregon. It's where your life is. It's where all the people you care about live. It's your home. And it's where you should be."

Kelli stared down at the soggy tissue in her hands. "I care about you too."

"Then go back to school. Go do all those things I can't do."

"What about these next two weeks?" Kelli switched tacks.

"We'll have a good time. Just like we used to have together."

Kelli eyed April skeptically. "Right. We'll have a great time thinking that this is the last time we'll ever be together."

"I don't like it either," April said sharply. "But I can't make it go away. It's hard enough watching my parents going crazy over it. I don't need to see you suffering too. I—I need to have fun, Kelli. I need to concentrate on something besides what's happening to me."

This was the argument that persuaded Kelli. April saw acquiescence on her friend's face. "We'll go into the city. We'll spend a few days at my mother's. Her place is small, but it's in SoHo and there's a million things to do, lots of places to go."

"We'll be like Siamese twins," April said. "Joined at the hip."

Kelli gave her a bittersweet look. "Until we're surgically separated," she said. "Or whatever it is doctors do with twins who share one heart."

Kelli's mother welcomed them, hurrying off to her job in the mornings and letting the girls sleep in. They roused themselves by midmorning, then set out with an agenda to do only the things they felt like doing. They spent two full days browsing department stores and boutiques, trying on the choicest clothing, the most fashionable wardrobes. On another day they ate lunch in Central

Park on a blanket under a tree, rode the subway from one end of one route to the other, and spent the rest of the rainy day in a giant bookstore in Times Square.

They spent a day at a trendy beauty salon, where Kelli had her dark hair streaked with bright fuchsia and April considered cutting hers but chickened out at the last minute. She opted instead for a rainbow manicure, having every fingernail painted a different color. They pierced their ears in three more places and bought diamond studs at Tiffany's for every new hole. They had tattoos put on their ankles. Kelli chose a dolphin and April a hibiscus. "It reminds me of the islands," she said.

One night Kelli's mother brought home a gorgeous arrangement of tropical flowers—orange-hued bird-of-paradise, red and yellow hibiscus, pale pink and lavender orchids, and snow-white gardenias. April sat it on the kitchen table and stared at it all evening. The scent was heavenly, and when she closed her eyes she could almost see the turquoise ocean and smell the salt-tinged air. And she could see Brandon's face, sun-browned, his hair bleached blond, his eyes as blue as the sky.

April told Kelli about her love of sailing, describing the sound the wind makes as it billows out the sails, the sharp snap the nylon makes when the boat comes about. "That settles it," Kelli said. "Whenever I get married, I'm going to demand a honeymoon in St. Croix."

"Lots of people do." April told her about the wedding gazebo she'd seen with Brandon.

"Sounds like heaven."

"Just like heaven." Afterward, April grew quiet, and that night she went to bed early, choosing not to stay up and watch the video she and Kelli had rented that afternoon.

As their two weeks together passed, April began to experience more frequent episodes of vertigo. One day she couldn't even get out of bed. Kelli sat by her bedside, and they played cards and board games. April kept losing her concentration and had to give it up when she started having double vision. Kelli asked if she should call April's parents, but April refused adamantly. The following day April seemed fine.

Two days before Kelli was scheduled to return to college, they stayed at April's for one final sleepover. "I'm going to miss you," April told Kelli in the privacy of April's bedroom after dinner with her parents.

"I can cancel my ticket. Just say the word."

"You've seen how it's going to be for me. Once I start getting worse, I won't even know you're in the same room. Believe me, it's better that you remember the fun we've had. Not the bad stuff."

Kelli turned her head, and April knew her friend didn't want her to see any tears. April got up from where they were sitting on the floor and went to her closet. "There's something I want you to have," she said. She disappeared into the walk-in closet and emerged dragging an enormous box.

Kelli's eyes widened. "Big box."

April plopped it in front of her. "Open it."

Kelli lifted the lid, pushed aside layers of tissue, and gasped. "It's your wedding dress."

"It's yours now."

"But I can't—"

"Yes you can. We're the same size. At least we were until I started this stupid medication. I know it'll fit you. Try it on." April stood and lifted the ivory-colored gown, wrapped in tissue, from the box. "Please, Kelli."

Mutely Kelli stood, slipped off her night-shirt, and slid on the undergarments that April offered her one by one from her dresser drawer. When Kelli was sheathed in silk, April helped her into the magnificent dress. Seed pearls, sequins and lace, and layers of satin caught the lamp's light and gleamed. April fluffed the skirt, pulled the train so that it flowed behind Kelli on the carpet, and stepped aside. "Look," she said, nodding toward the full-length mirror on her wall.

Kelli stared at her reflection. The cut of the dress made her waist look tiny. Her trembling hands smoothed the bodice. "It's the most beautiful . . ." Her voice broke as words failed her.

April watched her friend and felt a lump rise in her throat as she remembered the day she had worn it for Mark. "Till death do us part," she had whispered to him. And death had parted them quickly.

"I don't even have a fiancé," Kelli said, her gaze never leaving the mirror.

"You will someday. It would make me very

happy to know that you wore this dress on your wedding day. I'll make sure Mom knows you're to get it. She'll put it into special storage until you're ready for it." April paused. "It's important to me, Kelli. I want you to have it."

Tears slid down Kelli's cheeks. "It will be an honor to wear this dress in your memory."

April stepped behind her and gazed at both their images in the glass—Kelli dark-eyed, dark-haired; April with a mane of red hair and light blue eyes. Their reflection reminded her of a superimposed pair of photographs, of two images slightly misaligned: Kelli alive and vibrant, April pale and other-worldly. Like a ghost staring over the shoulder of her friend.

She did not go to the airport to see Kelli off, but once Kelli had flown away, April felt desolate and friendless. And she kept experiencing dizzy spells, nausea, and more slurring of her speech. A woman from hospice who'd lost a son to cancer came for a visit, and April's parents made arrangements to convert the dining room into a sickroom. And finally one morning she sat upright in bed as her words to Kelli about sitting around in some kind of deathwatch came back to her. She had bid goodbye to everything and everyone who had meant anything to her in New York. She padded downstairs into the breakfast room, where her parents sat. They glanced up, startled by her sudden appearance.

"Honey, are you all right?" her mother asked, springing up to take her hand.

"I want to go back to St. Croix," April said. "That's where I want it to happen. Please, Daddy, please, take me back there right away."

15

Brandon had taken up the habit of driving into the hills whenever he got off work. He couldn't explain why he often took a route that caused him to pass in front of the house April and her family had once rented, but he did. The real estate agent had come and lowered the storm awnings over all the windows and arranged for a gardener to keep the bushes and hedges trimmed. The place looked deserted and forlorn, empty of life and activity. Some days Brandon sat in his parked car staring at the house. And brooding.

He never understood why April had left without a single word of goodbye. Neither, in the weeks that she'd been gone, did he understand why she'd never once attempted to call or write to him. He had misjudged her. He'd fooled himself into thinking she'd cared more about him than she really had. At first he'd been angry, but his anger had faded. Now he felt only disappointment and the keen edge of loneliness. It cut through him like a knife. Everyplace he went held some memory of her. He wished he could eradicate every trace of her from his mind and heart, but he couldn't. He had loved her, and she'd hurt him—without reason or provocation.

He reviewed their days together a hundred times in his thoughts, but he could think of nothing he might have said or done to make her shun him so completely. He'd saved her note, expecting some explanation of her "family problems," but when none came, the cold truth dawned on him. She didn't care about him. She never really had.

He felt that his life was unraveling, just as it had when his mother killed herself. Losing a girl was not the same as losing his mother, but the end result was the same. He was alone with no explanations, no understanding. His inner turmoil made him decide to wait until the winter term before heading off to college. He knew he couldn't handle the pressure right now. For once, his father was in agreement with him. After Brandon's announcement, his father told him, "You're only eighteen. Hang around. Work. Go away in January."

One afternoon in the middle of September, Brandon drove past the house and saw a workman on a ladder raising the awnings. He stopped his car and got out. "What's up?" he called.

"The place is rented," the man answered in his lilting island dialect.

"Do you know who's taking it?"

"No, man. The office did not tell me. They just sent to have the house opened and aired."

It pained Brandon that someone besides April would live there. In his mind it would always be her place.

Days later, unable to stem his curiosity, he again drove past the house. This time it looked occupied, although he couldn't see any of the occupants. After work on Saturday, he went hiking up in the hills near the house. By the time he'd reached a hill's summit, clouds had cluttered the sky and hidden the sun. He looked down at the house and saw into the cove, saw the wooden stairs leading to the beach, saw someone lying on a beach chair. He'd brought binoculars and aimed them at the person in the chair. The sun peeked out from behind a cloud bank, and light caught and glinted off a girl's red hair. His heart leaped into his throat.

It was April. She had returned and not told him. Sudden, blinding anger welled up inside him. She wasn't going to get away with it! She wasn't going to sneak in and out of his island, his life, at will, with no regard for his feelings. Determined to confront her, he half-jogged, half-slid down the long trail, through the underbrush, to the top of the stairs, and down the stairs to the sandy beach.

April must have heard him coming because she sat up and watched him approach along the final few yards between the stairs and her chair. Her hair was tied back and held with a scrunchie; her eyes were calm and clear, not at all surprised by his appearance. His heart thudded as he stood over her chair, panting with the exertion of the run, his shirt sticking to his back, sweat running down his face.

"Hello, Brandon," she said quietly. "I've been expecting you."

Her greeting startled and silenced him. He regained his composure quickly and, in a voice dripping with sarcasm, said, "Well, I wasn't expecting you."

"I know you're mad at me."

"No joke."

"You're mad because I left without ever telling you goodbye. I know it wasn't very nice of me, but I had good reasons for leaving."

"Such as?"

"I was sick."

"And now you're all better?" He kept the sarcasm in his tone. She didn't look sick.

April stood, somewhat unsteadily. "Can we walk down the beach while we talk?"

He studied her more closely and saw that she looked puffy and a little dazed. For the first time, his anger wavered. "After you."

"Could I hold on to your arm?"

He let her take hold of him and was surprised by how clumsily she moved. Yet her hand felt warm and familiar. The scent of her skin and hair reminded him of their summer afternoons together, filling him with the old

longing to hold her in his arms. "All right, so
I believe you. You've been sick." He remembered the day they'd gone on the picnic.
"Has it got something to do with that day we
went sailing?"

"Yes."

By now his anger had evaporated. Dread
arrived to take its place. "So what was
wrong?"

"The same thing that was wrong when I
first came to St. Croix." Her gait was awkward, but still she walked along the edge of
the water, her delicate painted toes washed
by small lapping waves.

"You never said anything to me about your
being sick," he said suspiciously. "We were
together plenty, so it's not like you couldn't
have said something before now."

"No, I never told you."

He stopped walking and looked down at
the top of her bowed head. Except for that
one day they'd gone snorkeling, she had
seemed happy and healthy to him all the time
they'd been together. "And so that's why
you left? Because you got sick? St. Croix has
doctors, you know."

"I went back to New York to see my doctor. I've been under his care for a time, and he knew my case very well."

"So what did he tell you?"

"He repeated some tests."

"He did?" Brandon knew he wasn't asking the most obvious question of all—*"What's wrong with you?"*—because he couldn't bring himself to say the words. He knew in his gut something bad was wrong, and he really didn't want to hear it. It had been easier when he'd thought she'd gone away without a word because she hadn't truly cared about him. Then he could be angry at her, dislike her, think of her as inconsiderate and selfish. But now he was discovering she wasn't any of those things. Now she was telling him that she'd had a terrible reason for going.

"Yes. After the tests, he told me . . . us, my parents and me . . . that I still had an inoperable brain tumor. That the tumor was growing once again. That I probably only had about two to three months to live." Her voice never quavered. She said the words quietly and without emotion.

For Brandon, time stood still. The world stopped spinning, the waves stopped rolling, the sun stopped shining. Only once before in his life had such a phenomenon happened to him.

Brandon rushed into the kitchen, books in hand, ready to seize an apple and head out again. He skidded to a stop because his father was standing at the counter, his face pale as paste. "What's wrong?" Brandon asked.

"Your mother took the boat out this morning."

Brandon's heart froze. "Has something happened to her?"

"She killed herself, son."

"Liar!" He lunged at his father.

His father held up a piece of paper. "It's true. She left us a note."

Brandon grabbed the paper. He felt the world stop turning as he read her words of farewell.

Now, to April, he said, "You have a *brain tumor*? I thought Mark was the one who was sick."

Her gaze found his. Her eyes were incredibly clear, their expression absolutely serious. "Mark and I met in the hospital. We were both patients. He saw me through my radiation treatments. My doctors had hoped that the tumor would shrink, that they could do gamma knife surgery on it. It didn't. They couldn't. But at that time it had stopped growing. And so Mark and I planned to be married, to get on with our lives. Except he had the car crash and died."

Although she had told Brandon about Mark already, hearing it in the context of her own illness made it especially heart-wrenching. "Why didn't you tell me sooner? You should have said something before now."

She gazed out at the sea. He watched her face and realized she was having trouble con-centrating. He knew he shouldn't press her, but he couldn't help it. He had to know. With effort, she said, "I didn't know how to tell you. You were so hurt about your mother, I didn't want to hurt you any more." She paused, then turned back to face him. "But it was for selfish reasons too. I wanted so much to be all right. You were so nice to me. I wanted you to remember me as someone you had fun with . . . someone you passed one very special summer with. I didn't want to be sick. I didn't want to be pitied. I wanted exactly what you gave me—a wonderful time. Thank you."

"Why did you come back now to St. Croix?" His heart pounded and his stomach tightened because he already knew the answer.

"It's a beautiful place to die. It's where I want to die."

Her speech had slowed, slurred. Emotion clogged his throat, tightening around it like a noose. His arms shot around her, and he held her close against his chest. He stroked her hair, pulling off the band, letting the red-gold mass fall and catch the breeze. He kissed the crown of her head and lifted her, carrying her to the stairs. He heard footsteps and looked up to see her mother clattering down toward them, anxiously asking, "Is she all right?"

April wound her arms around Brandon's neck and lifted her head so that she could see her mother. "I'm . . . all right," she managed.

But Brandon knew it was a lie. She wasn't all right. And she never would be again.

Once April was settled in her room, Brandon sat on the sofa with Janice. A storm had come up, and rain pelted the French doors, smashing leaves and flower petals into the glass. He thought back to that first night when he'd stopped by to see April . . . the girl from the hilltop, spinning in the sunlight, sending a balloon skyward to celebrate the memory of a dead love.

"I'm glad you understand why she left without a word," Janice was telling him. "She never meant to hurt you."

"I know that now," Brandon answered. "What's going to happen to her?"

"She'll steadily decline. Coma, then death."

"How long?"

"As long as it takes."

He felt sick to his stomach. "It's hard to believe."

"We've hired a nurse who'll come by every day, see to her medical needs. There won't be many."

"There's a good hospital in Christiansted."

Janice shook her head. "That's not what April wants. And it wouldn't make any difference anyway. Her father and I want her to have things exactly her way."

A clap of thunder startled them both.

Brandon turned. "Can I . . . do you mind if I sort of hang around with her?"

Janice studied him. "Why?"

"Because I care about her. Because I want to say goodbye." He thought about his mother. He'd never been able to tell her goodbye. "I know I'm not family. But I won't get in your way, and it will mean everything to me if I can be with her until . . . well, you know."

"Will your father mind?"

"I think he'll understand." Watching April's mother, seeing her sadness, her helplessness, helped Brandon realize that his mother had abandoned both him and his father. April had told him his father hadn't been to blame, but he'd fought with her about it. Brandon swept his fingers through his hair. "Please, let me be with her."

"Her dying won't be easy to watch."

"Believe me, I know."

"Yes . . . I suppose you do."

They said nothing more, only sat and watched the storm hurl its fury at the garden outside.

16

Later that night, when Brandon told his father about April, Bill Benedict stared in disbelief. "Are you serious? Why, that's terrible. Terrible! She's so young and pretty and with her whole life in front of her. How can this be?"

Brandon had figured that the news would affect his father but was surprised by the intensity of his reaction. "I didn't believe it at first, but I talked to her mother and there's nothing more the doctors can do."

"I know this girl is special to you, son. I'm sorry for your sake too."

A surge of emotion clogged Brandon's throat. He cleared it away. "Yes . . . she's pretty special to me."

His father began to pace the floor. "Her poor parents. They must be devastated. I liked the whole family. The way they came to your graduation and all—well, that was really nice of them. Hugh and I talked business for more than an hour. Listen, if there's anything they need or want, you let me know. I'd like to help out."

"You would?"

He stopped his restless pacing. "Of course I would. They're strangers here. They have no one to support them."

Until then, Brandon hadn't thought about April's parents' position. He'd been concentrating on April, and on his own feelings. But his father was correct; the Lancasters didn't have anyone in St. Croix to call on. "I'll tell them you'd like to help."

"I might have thought that April would have wanted to be in her home back in the States. Why did she want her last days to be in St. Croix?"

"She's always loved it here," Brandon said. "I don't know. Maybe it's because choosing your place to die might be the only thing a person has control over. Sort of like Mom did, I guess." The comment had simply spilled out of Brandon. He hadn't meant anything mean or cruel by it. He was really discussing April, not his mother.

His father measured him carefully with a look. "She did pick her time to die, all right."

"I didn't mean—"

His father waved him off. "Forget it. No matter what you think, Brandon, I couldn't have stopped your mother from doing what she did. She'd been clinically depressed for years, but she wouldn't go get help for it."

Clinically depressed? It was the first time he'd heard the term used in conjunction with his mother. "She was?"

"Surely you noticed that she was different, that she wasn't like your friends' mothers." His father's tone sounded acidic.

It was true. Sometimes she'd slept away entire days, then stayed up, wandering around the house all night. And of course, there'd been her drinking. "I—I always knew she wasn't happy."

"And you figured it was my fault, or perhaps even your fault."

Brandon felt his face color but didn't comment.

"It was *her* fault, son. She drank booze and popped pills to escape from real life. I couldn't stop her. Don't you think I tried?"

His father's words echoed what Brandon had said to April when they'd talked about his mother's suicide—that Brandon had tried to help her but couldn't. "You were gone most of the time," Brandon said stubbornly, feeling as if he needed to somehow defend his mother's actions. "She was always alone. That depressed her."

"We've been over that before." His father's voice grew cool. "She was the same whether I was around or not."

Brandon sighed. He didn't want to rehash the past or any of its old arguments. Tonight shouldn't be about his mother's death. Or his and his father's problems. Tonight should be about April, the girl he loved, who was dying. "Look, Dad, I don't want to argue with you. Right now, it means a lot to me that you want to help April and her parents through this bad time. I appreciate it, and they will too."

His father offered a tentative smile. "Good. I don't want to argue with you either. But I really meant what I said earlier.

Have her family call me if they want anything. I know plenty of people in the islands,
and they'd be happy to pitch in."

"I don't think I'd spread around too much
information about them. I mean, they're private people and they wouldn't like a lot of
attention. At least, not for April's sake."

"I know what you're saying. Don't worry,
I'll be discreet. Nobody wants a bunch of
strangers in their faces no matter how well-
intentioned their motives."

In his father's statement, Brandon recognized the man's own philosophy—after the
suicide, he'd shut everybody out, even Brandon. "I may want to quit my job to be with
April," Brandon said. "Not right away, but
as she gets worse. So that means that I won't
be saving as much money for college and all
as I told you I would."

"It doesn't matter. The job, the money—
they were for your sake, not mine. I always
found work to be therapeutic. I'd hoped you
might find it to be the same."

Brandon's father escaped into work to dis-
tract himself, but Brandon knew that he
couldn't do things that way. He wanted to
saturate himself in April's presence, hold on

to her for as long as he could. He told his father good night and went to his room, walking down the long hall that led past what had once been his parents' bedroom, where he paused. He resisted the urge to open the door and look inside. Throughout his life, he'd come home many an afternoon to find his mother holed up inside that bedroom. She would be lying on the bed, the room darkened, the pillows propped to elevate her head and shoulders. The TV would be on at low volume in the corner, a glass and a bottle of whiskey on the nightstand. She might wave him inside, she might not. If he came in, she would cling to him, her breath smelling of whiskey, and she would cry and dump her misery on him.

Yet right now, despite all her shortcomings, Brandon longed to see his mother, tell her about April and hear words of sympathy. He inched past the room, then walked rapidly around the corner and into his own room, the ghost of his mother's memory following along behind.

Over the following weeks, Brandon grew respectful of his father for the things he did to help April's parents. He often had dinner sent up for them from the best restaurants in Christiansted. A ring of the doorbell and a delivery-truck driver would be on the front steps with packages of hot food. "How kind and thoughtful," Janice always told Brandon.

His father insisted that April's father go golfing with him. "You're a phone call away on our cell phones," Bill would reason. "The golf course is less than twenty minutes from the house. Plus, Brandon's here. He can handle any emergency until we get back."

It pleased Brandon that his father considered him capable of handling any emergency, even though he hoped he wouldn't have to handle one. He loved April and respected her parents immensely; he didn't want to ever let them down.

On her good days, Brandon helped April down to the beach, where she'd lie in the beach chair, facing the sea, holding his hand and drifting in and out of sleep. She slept a lot. But sometimes she'd have better days, when she was more alert, not nauseated, and able to concentrate. He waited patiently for those days, praying for them, enjoying them when they came to her.

One afternoon while they were together on the patio under a canopy, out of the heat of the sun, April in a lounge chair, Brandon beside her in another, she awoke, stretched, and asked, "Are you still here?"

"Where else would I be?"

"Sailing? Out having fun?"

"I want to be here. With you."

"This is very kind of you, Brandon."

"I don't do it to be kind. I'm not into good deeds, and you're not a charity case."

"Still, you don't have to spend all your free time with me."

"Says who?" He pulled his sunglasses down the bridge of his nose and peered over them at her. "You getting tired of me? You trying to let me down easy? Get rid of me?"

She giggled, and the sound pleased him immensely. "You're silly. I'd never want to get rid of you."

"Same here," he told her softly.

She turned her face away. "You never told me why you didn't go away to school the way you were planning to."

He repositioned his sunglasses to cover his eyes. "I'm not sure myself. There was just so much to think about—packing up most everything I owned, trading living in my house for a dorm room. I just wasn't ready. I'll go in January." *After you're gone,* he told himself.

"Where will you go? Did you pick a place where it snows?"

He shook his head. "No snow. I've decided on Texas A&M. Maybe I'll major in landscape architecture. I like working outside. And I like to make plants grow."

She reached over and squeezed his hand. "You'll be good at it. But for right now, I'm glad you're here, and so is my mom. I think she really likes having you around."

"Seriously? I don't want to be in the way."

"You aren't in anybody's way."

"Your mom's a great mom," he said. "She talks to me like I'm a person, not some dopey kid."

"Is that the way your mom talked to you? Like you were dumb?"

He shook his head sadly. "We'd talk sometimes, but mostly she cried."

"So does mine. I hear her at night sometimes."

"Your mom has a reason to cry. Mine just

cried." Remembering was painful because it made him feel so helpless. "Some days I'd come home from school and she'd be locked in her room. Some days I'd come home and she'd almost pounce on me and ask a million questions. It wasn't so much that she was interested in my life, but that her life was so horrible that mine seemed great by comparison. It's like she got her excitement through me. What's that called?"

"Vicariousness," April supplied.

"Except for when we all went sailing. She really loved that."

"I love sailing too."

He thought about his mother's choice of a place to die. If only she hadn't chosen their boat. If only she hadn't done it at all. "Is it as much fun as car racing?"

"It's quieter."

He smiled. Now she was careful not to mention Mark around him. Not that he would have minded anymore. Brandon was certain that she had feelings only for him. He knew he loved her and always would. He would go on living, and every day of his life he would remember her.

He reached over and laced his fingers through hers. "If you were strong enough to go sailing, I'd take you."

She shook her head. "I'd like to go, but I know I'd get sick."

"Do you hurt?"

"Not really." She repeated what Dr. Sorenson had told her about the brain and its inability to feel pain. "It's not much comfort, really. The dizzy spells make my stomach queasy, sort of like a permanent case of seasickness. That's why I stay in one position so much—to keep the dizziness away. I've been told that throwing up on a guy isn't very romantic."

He laughed out loud, amazed at her ability to make jokes. "Probably not."

She drifted off to sleep, and Brandon raised their joined hands and pressed his lips to her fingers. *I love you, April,* he said silently. *I love you so much.*

17

April hated the days when she could barely keep her eyes open. Sometimes she felt tangled in a thick clinging fog that clogged her memory and sapped her strength. It worried her that the stupor of perpetual drowsiness would push her into oblivion. She wasn't ready for oblivion yet. Some nights she set her alarm clock and put it under her pillow just so that she could hear it and struggle to the surface of sleep. As long as she could hear it ringing, turn it off, and listen to its ticking, she knew she hadn't passed into timelessness, into eternity.

She was rarely alone anymore. Her parents took turns sitting beside her bed. Her mother

read, her father arranged a makeshift desk
and did paperwork. Their presence brought
her comfort. She'd wake and sense that one
of them was there. The flutter of papers
meant her father. The occasional turning of a
book's page meant her mother. When April
was unable to come to the table for meals,
they brought their meals into her room. She
didn't eat much—no appetite. At some point,
the nurse (whom she recognized by her
quick, efficient movements) inserted an IV
into April's arm.

"For hydration," she heard the woman tell
her parents.

I'm drinking through a needle, she told
herself. *Yummy.*

Brandon often came to be with her too.
She liked that. He usually held her hand and
watched TV or videotapes, which her father
kept in good supply. The drone of the televi-
sion almost always meant that Brandon was
with her. On the days when she felt more
alert, she wanted to be taken down to the
beach, or at least outside to sit by the pool.
She found the sight of sunlight on water very
comforting. She didn't know why. And she
liked to talk, although her speech was often

slurred. Talking connected her with those she loved. She recalled Mark's struggle to talk during his last days, how he had fought to say everything that was in his heart. She felt the same way. If only she could push the contents of her mind into those surrounding her. If only she were telepathic.

One evening, when her parents were with her in the sickroom, she said, "I don't know how much longer I can stay awake."

"Don't try," her father said, easing onto the bed and touching her cheek. "You just sleep. Your mom and I'll be right here."

"That's not what I mean." Her mother and father glanced at each other questioningly. April tried again to express what she wanted to say. "I know I won't be waking up one of these times."

Her father's hand tightened on hers, and her mother shook her head. "Don't say such things. You've got plenty of time."

"No," April said. "No, I don't."

Neither one of them contradicted her.

"I want you to know," April said, every word a struggle, "that you're the best parents in the world. And I'm lucky to have had you for mine."

"And you're the best daughter," her father said, smoothing her thick red hair.

"We've been the lucky ones," her mother added.

"Would you rather have had a son?"

Her father drew back, a look of disdain on his face. "Are you joking? I always wanted a girl. From the time your mother and I were first married, I told her I wanted to be surrounded by beautiful women." He glanced at his wife. "Isn't that right, Janice? Didn't I always tell you I wanted a girl?"

"It's the truth," April's mother said. "Scout's honor."

"That's nice." April didn't know why she'd asked such a dumb question, but she appreciated their answer. "I wanted a boy," she said. "Even though Mark couldn't have children, I still would have wanted a son."

"You've given us all we ever wanted," her mother said. "Just not for long enough."

It was breaking April's heart to see her parents so sad. She asked, "Do you know, some of the best times I ever had were when I was growing up and we'd all go out to eat at those fancy restaurants. I felt so grown up sitting at the table with you both. I had my own wineglass filled with ginger ale. And you let me order peanut butter and jelly. It wasn't ever on the menu, but you made them fix it for me."

"The first time we took you out to dinner, you were two years old." Her father smiled, remembering. "You knocked over a water glass, then crawled beneath the table and played in the puddle."

Her mother shook her head in dismay. "I was embarrassed, but then I got the giggles and couldn't stop laughing. The maître d' looked as if he would have a heart attack. The very idea of our bringing a child into such a fancy place almost made him faint."

Seeing them smile over the shared memory made April feel good. They'd been sad for so long on her account. She didn't want them sad. "I guess we didn't go back there to eat again."

Her father snorted. "They acted as if a child were a parasite instead of a pleasure. No, I would never have taken you back to such a place."

Her mother patted April's arm. "We

waited until you were a bit more mature before we ventured into four-star dining again
with you, however."

"I remember my birthday party when I
was six. You took me to some restaurant that
had a dance floor and one of those balls that
spun overhead and sparkled all over us." She
looked at her father. "You danced with me."
She'd stood on his shoes and he'd twirled her
around the dance floor while a band played a
song she could still hear inside her head and
speckles of light spilled across them.

"Well, I couldn't very well step on your
toes," he said. "I would have squished
them."

"We'll never dance on my wedding day."
Her smile faded. "I didn't mean to say that.
I—I don't want you to feel bad."

Her mother turned her head aside. Her father rubbed his thumb across April's knuck-
les, over and over, as if touching her was
something he couldn't get enough of. "If I
could take your place now, baby, I would."

"No . . . that's not right. You need to
stay with Mother. It's a horrible thing to be
left alone." April brightened. "And don't
you worry about me. Mark's in heaven wait-

ing for me. Before he died, he told me he'd be waiting and watching for me to come to him. So, you see, I won't be alone. I have you and Mom on this side of life, and Mark on the other side. I'll be fine, Daddy. Really, I'll be fine."

"He'd better take good care of you. If not, he'll answer to me when I get there." Her father's voice was barely a whisper.

April's eyelids felt heavy, and concentrating was becoming more difficult. But she felt good that she had been able to tell her parents some of the things that were in her heart. To her mother, she said, "You remember about the wedding dress, don't you?"

"Yes. It belongs to Kelli."

April closed her eyes. The conversation had exhausted her, and sleepiness was beginning to shut down her ability to think and talk. "When Brandon comes, make sure he has some new movies to watch. He's seen the ones next to the TV set already."

"I'll take care of it," her father said.

His voice sounded as if it were coming through a long tunnel. "I think I'll take a little nap now," she said. She felt her mother kiss her cheek. "Is the moon out tonight?"

"Half a moon," her father said.

"Is it pretty on the water?"

"Beautiful."

April remembered parasailing, the sensation of flying, of looking down and seeing the world from a bird's-eye view. "Will you open my window? If I wake up late tonight, I want to see the moonlight. The moonbeams come into my room late at night, you know. They make a path on the water and on my carpet, and across my bed. Sometimes . . . I feel as if I could . . . get up . . . and walk straight up the path. Into heaven. Mommy, Daddy, I love you."

She felt her mother kiss her cheek as she tumbled into sleep.

18

The times when April was awake and aware were fewer and farther between. Every time she was asleep, Brandon would wonder if this might be the time she'd slip into a coma and not wake up. One afternoon her eyes fluttered open and she looked around the room as if she didn't recognize it. Anxiously Brandon leaned over her. "April? You okay? It's me."

Her gaze slowly locked onto his face. She blinked. "Brandon." Her smile was crooked, as if she couldn't control one side of her face. "How long have you been here?"

"Not long," he lied.

"Did I fall asleep? Sorry . . . rude of me."

"It doesn't matter."

"Is it raining?"

"A storm moved in about ten minutes ago." He moved aside so that she could see through the window facing the sea. Rain splattered the glass, and the sea was a froth of churning foam. "But you know how the weather is in the Caribbean. The sun will be out again in no time."

"That's good. I love the sun."

She didn't say anything else for such a long time that he thought she'd fallen back to sleep, but she finally said, "I want to tell you something."

"Tell me."

She held out her hand, and he took hold of it. Her skin felt cool and dry. "Did you know that I love you?"

His heart skipped.

"It's true. But *shhh* . . . don't tell Mark. It would make him sad." She was talking as if Mark were alive in the room with them. Brandon felt a prickly sensation up his spine. Mark was waiting for her. She would cross over to him and he would have her forever. Would April meet Brandon's mother? Was there a place in heaven for those who had shed life like a piece of clothing? "If you see my mother—"

"I'll tell her you love her. And that you forgive her."

Tears burned and brimmed and stung his eyes. "Yes . . . I forgive her," Brandon said, hardly trusting his voice. "I love you, April."

"Aren't I lucky? I've been twice loved. Don't let anyone tell you that you can't love two people with all your heart." She turned her head so that she could see Mark's photograph on the bedside table. "Mark, this is Brandon. And I love him." She turned her eyes back to Brandon. "Now, you go find someone else to love too. Please."

"I don't want—"

"*Shhh.* We don't always get what we want." She drifted away from him, back into her blanket of fog, to the world of semiconsciousness where he could not follow.

Later he returned to the living room. April's mother was sitting on the sofa, looking out at the sea and the driving rain sweeping past the plate glass window in sheets. The world looked gray and soggy; even the palm fronds battered by the whipping wind were a dull green. She turned when she heard him, and her eyes were as colorless as the rain, as dull as the leaden clouds. She asked, "Is she sleeping?"

"Yes. She fell asleep a while ago. But I didn't want to leave her."

"I know what you mean."

He lowered himself to the love seat that butted up against one arm of the sofa, feeling totally helpless, unable to find words to comfort either April's mother or himself.

"I still can't believe she's dying," April's mother said. "It makes no sense to me. Parents aren't supposed to outlive their children." He winced. She paled. "Oh, Brandon, I'm sorry. That was so insensitive of me."

"But it's true. Even if a parent chooses to die. It's more natural than for the child to die first." He stared out at the driving rain, at the whitecaps skidding across the surface of the sea in the distance. "Did you know that if you dive down deep under the ocean, you can't even tell if there's a storm on the top side? It's quiet in the deep. And cold. When I saw my mother in the casket, I touched her. She was ice-cold. All the warmth had leaked out of her, the way sand oozes through your fingers underwater. I can't stand to think of April that way." His voice grew softer and faded.

"I can't stand it either. When she was five, when they first discovered her tumor, I used to stand beside her hospital bed and hold on to her even while she slept. I guess I thought that as long as I held on, death couldn't come for her. Or that if it did, it would have to bump me out of the way and I could grab it, throttle it, throw it out of her room. But death isn't something that comes from the outside. I think it lives in all of us and it lies in wait, like a lion crouching near its prey. Then, when our guard is down, our body defenseless because of disease or trauma or inconsolable bad feelings like your mother's, death comes out and stakes its claim."

Brandon told himself that if she was correct, nothing could drive death out. It had to leave on its own accord. And when it did leave, it took life with it and left behind body shells, just as sea creatures vacated outgrown shells, leaving the old ones abandoned on the ocean floor. "Do you know that I think April is the prettiest girl I ever saw? I'll never forget the color of her hair. Where'd she get it from? Neither you nor her father has red hair."

Janice smiled. "My great-grandmother came over from England and married a New Yorker. She was renowned for her beauty. And her hair of red gold." Her smile faded. "Corrine—that was her name—lost three babies. One to diphtheria. One to pneumonia. One to measles. Diseases that we banish now with injections and antibiotics. I wonder if they'll ever have an inoculation against cancer? Against death?"

Or against a person wanting to die? he wondered. "It must have been hard to bury so many babies," he said, thinking of April's great-great-grandmother.

"Nothing can be harder than burying your children," Janice said.

"Burying a mother is pretty hard too."

"That's true. My mother died when I was thirty-five, my father when I was forty, and it was difficult to lose them. I'm so sorry you had to go through that so young."

He stood and walked over to the glass door. The storm had stopped, but the sun had not yet emerged and the world looked flat and dull. He shoved his hands deep into the pockets of his shorts and rocked back on his heels. "I still wonder why," he said, barely aware that he'd even spoken. "Her note said life hurt too much . . . as if that's a reason. I see April and I know how much she wants to live. It makes no sense to me that someone like my mother wouldn't want to live. You know?"

"It doesn't make any sense to me either," Janice told him.

He looked down and blinked against moisture that had filled his eyes, embarrassed at having said so much to April's mother concerning his most private feelings. "Sorry. I don't mean to talk so much."

"It's okay, Brandon. Really. I only wish I could answer your questions. The truth is, no one knows how another person truly feels because we can't walk around in each other's skins." She got up from the sofa and stood beside him, gazing out the glass door with him. "But I do know one thing. I know that she had one fine son."

He glanced at Janice, saw that her ex-

pression was kind and sincere. He felt his
cheeks redden. "That's nice of you to
say."

"It's the truth. I would have been proud
to have called you my son."

"Thanks."

"I mean it."

"You should have had lots of children.
Tons of them."

She laughed. "I always thought so too."

The sun suddenly broke through the bank
of billowing gray clouds, hurling breathtak-
ing shafts of light into the sea. The water
turned from gray to green where the light
penetrated, as if some alien's spaceship were
anchored beneath the surface. With the sight
came a feeling of hope to Brandon. Here, in
this house, standing beside the mother of the
girl he loved, he felt a sense of peace and be-
longing. He couldn't stop time. He couldn't
turn it back. All he had was this precious slice
of it, and it felt good to be alive.

Early the next morning, as Brandon drove up
to the house, he saw an ambulance sitting in
the driveway, its red light swirling and casting
eerie reflections on the surrounding trees and

brush. It punctuated the gray morning light with urgency. All was silent. Brandon cut off his engine, flung open the car door, and raced up to the house. The front door was ajar, and he hurried inside. April's father stood in the living room in his bathrobe and bare feet. He looked up, and his face was haggard and creased by grief. He said, "She's gone."

"Gone?"

"She died in her sleep. The paramedics are with her, but there's nothing they can do. My little girl is gone. Gone."

Brandon's back stiffened and, without comment, he edged out the front door and walked quickly into the surrounding woods, heedless of the wet foliage slapping against his arms and legs as he plowed deeper into the jungle. When he came to a small clearing he stopped, turned his face skyward, and screamed.

19

April Lancaster was going home.

Brandon stood on the tarmac along with his father and April's parents at the St. Croix airport, next to the jet plane that was to take April and her family away. A long black hearse drove through the security gates toward them. The baggage handlers, who'd been busy tossing luggage onto the conveyor belt, ceased their activity as the hearse stopped beside the plane. Pallbearers from the local funeral home got out of the vehicle, opened the back, and slid out a rolling cart that held a long pink casket trimmed in silver and with silver handles. Flecks of metallic paint caught the morning sun and glittered like jewels.

Brandon was grateful that his father had pulled strings to allow the four of them to stand out on the loading area, so close to the casket. As the men rolled the casket toward the conveyor belt, April's mother stepped forward. She touched the hard shell that held her daughter's body, leaned forward, and kissed it. Brandon's throat constricted, and he forced his gaze away. The sadness was as heavy as the humid tropical air that surrounded them.

Because the St. Croix airport was so small, he could hear taxi horns and the voices and laughter of tourists as they prepared to board the flight and return to the States. At the end of the single runway the sea sparkled, and in the other direction hills rose, lush and green. He returned his gaze to the casket and saw the pallbearers lift it onto the conveyor belt. The belt moved forward, and the glittering pink casket slid upward into the dark belly of the plane.

He knew this was April's wish—to return to New York and be buried beside Mark Gianni, the man she had chosen in life to be with forever. At least in death, she could have her final wish. Moisture filled his eyes, and the casket became blurred. He felt April's mother take his hand.

"I guess that's it. I guess it's our turn to get on board now."

He couldn't see her eyes hidden behind the dark glasses but saw the tracks of tears along her cheeks. "I guess so."

April's father put his arm around her shoulders, as if to hold her up, and put out his hand to Brandon's father. "Bill, thanks for everything. You made a lot of things go more smoothly for us and I'm grateful for that. If you're ever in New York . . ."

"Sure. I'll call."

Hugh turned to Brandon and extended his hand. "You're a fine young man, Brandon. I'm glad we had the opportunity to know you. In spite of the circumstances."

Brandon nodded, not trusting his voice.

April's mother hugged him, and he hugged her hard in return. Everything was slipping away from him. He couldn't hold on to anything he loved. "You take care of yourself," she said. "You have a great time in college, and send us an invitation to your graduation, because we'll come. It's a promise."

"Sure," he managed.

The four of them walked back inside the airport, and when the boarding call came, Brandon waved April's parents into the plane. All around them, tourists chattered and dragged bags loaded with souvenirs of the islands. All Brandon wanted to do was get away from them. Didn't they know what was going on? Didn't they realize that April was dead and that he hurt so badly that he could hardly breathe?

Outside, in the bright September sun, he fumbled for his sunglasses. He stood beside his father, and together they watched the large jet back away from the gate, taxi down the runway, rev its engines, and gather speed. The air was split by the roar of jets, saturated by the smell of hot fuel. Slowly the plane lifted, a silver bird headed to another time and place. Brandon watched until it disappeared behind a bank of snow-white cumulus clouds. And out of his life. He felt his father's hand on his shoulder.

"Son," he heard his father say.

"What?" Brandon felt desolate.

"I, um, was wondering if maybe we could have lunch together."

"I'm not hungry. And it's only ten-thirty."

"Well, I was wondering something else too."

Brandon removed his sunglasses and stared straight into his father's face. His father looked nervous, anxious. "What else?"

"A couple of weeks ago—when I knew this day was coming for you—I had the boat taken out of dry dock."

Brandon felt a flush radiate through his body. "You did?"

"It's down at the marina in its regular slip, and I was thinking that if you would like to, we could take it out this afternoon. Just the two of us. It's been a while, but I thought it was something we could do. I mean, that is, if you want."

The boat. Their boat. His mother's boat. Longing filled him. He wanted to feel the wind in his face. He wanted to taste the salt air. He wanted to touch the decks, the galley, the chairs where his mother had last been. In his father's eyes, he saw uncertainty. A tremor flickered along his rigidly held jaw as he waited for Brandon's answer.

His father added, "I was also thinking it

might be good for us to take some time together . . . take the boat around to some of
the cays and islands. You don't head off for
school until January, and I'd like to take
about a month off from work and spend it
sailing. You don't have to decide right now,
but would you think about it?"

Brandon understood that his father was
reaching out to him, wanted to make things
right between them. He wasn't sure what *he*
wanted, but he did know he was tired of feeling angry and resentful. "I'd like to go sailing
today," he said. "I'll think about the other."

His father grinned and nodded profusely.
"Good! Very, very good, son. So let's go
home, change, and head to the marina."

"I'll meet you there," Brandon said. "In a
couple of hours. There's something I have to
do first."

"All right." His father looked at his watch.
"See you at, say . . . one o'clock?"

"I'll be there."

An hour later, Brandon drove his car to the
now vacant house where April had once lived.
He parked, got out, and started up the hill
behind the house. At the crest of the hill he

stood, catching his breath and gazing out at the bright blue Caribbean sea. A breeze lifted his hair off his brow. *Good,* he thought. He'd hoped for a good stiff breeze.

He reached into his back pocket, pulled out a red balloon, and filled it with air. He tied it off, reached back into his pocket, pulled out a yellow ribbon, and tied it onto the balloon. Then he raised his hands over his head and let go. The ribbon trailed against his arm, and he resisted the urge to grab hold and not release it. By letting it go, he was letting April go too. He was telling her good-bye. He was giving her to Mark. Forever.

He shielded his eyes and watched as the balloon drifted higher and higher against the vast blue sky.

To find out more about April Lancaster
and Mark Gianni, turn the page
for a sneak preview of
Lurlene McDaniel's companion
to this book,
Till Death Do Us Part.

0-553-57085-4

On sale now from Bantam Books.

Till Death Do Us Part
by Lurlene McDaniel

Published by
Bantam Doubleday Dell Publishing Group, Inc.
1540 Broadway
New York, New York 10036

An excerpt from *Till Death Do Us Part* by Lurlene McDaniel:

"That guy's staring at you again, April."

April Lancaster didn't need Kelli to tell her that the boy on the far side of the hospital's patient rec room was looking at her. She could almost *feel* his gaze. She had been in the hospital for two days and he'd been stealing glances at her every time she ventured out of her room. "Ignore him," April whispered to Kelli. "I do."

"But why? He's cute. Even if he is too skinny for my taste."

"This isn't a social club, Kelli. It's a hospital. I didn't come here to meet guys."

"Well, I say why let a good opportunity slip away?"

April shook her head. "You're impossible."

Her best friend grinned. "I'm only trying to cheer you up. Take your mind off this whole thing. And if you meet a cute guy in the bargain, then what's the harm?"

April pointedly twisted in the lounge chair so that her back was to the boy. She didn't want to be stared at, and she certainly didn't want to meet some guy who was sick. She figured he had to be sick; why else would he be a patient in this huge New York City medical complex?

Kelli interrupted her thoughts. "What is going on with you? Medically, I mean. When can you leave?"

The last thing April wanted to do was dwell on the frightening possibilities as to why she was in the hospital. "I'm only here for testing," she said. "I'm sure I'll be out by the end of the week."

"But by then spring break will be over. We leave tomorrow, and the weatherman said an inch of fresh powder is falling in Vermont as we speak. This might be the last chance for a ski trip this year."

April and her friends had been planning

the trip for weeks. It was supposed to be part of her birthday present. And since it was their senior year, it would be their final spring break together as a group. "I can't help it," she said gloomily. "Even if my doctor releases me earlier, my parents wouldn't let me go."

"Why not?"

April didn't want to say. Not while there was so much speculation about the origins of her numbing headaches. The headaches had built in intensity for the past several months, causing her to get dizzy, even sick to her stomach. When she'd passed out from the pain in school two days earlier, her parents had hustled her out of their Long Island community and into a hospital in the city. The headaches could still be nothing.

Or they could be the other thing. The "thing" she had decided *not* to discuss with Kelli. "Oh, you know my parents. They fall to pieces if I have a hangnail. Besides, Dad won't let me drive from New York to Vermont by myself."

Kelli chewed her bottom lip. "I could wait till you're released. Then you and I could drive up together."

"No way." April shook her head. "Kelli, I appreciate it, but you go on with the others."

Kelli slumped in her chair, crossed her arms, and pouted. "It won't be the same without you there. This is our last spring break together."

April sighed, feeling disappointed too. "Maybe we can do something together our first spring break from college next year."

"Fat chance. We'll all be scattered to the ends of the earth."

"I'm sorry," April said softly, her eyes filling with tears.

Kelli scooted forward and seized April's hands. "Don't cry. I'm such a jerk for making you feel worse than you already do. Tell you what, we'll go to the shore this summer when all this is behind you. You've always liked the beach better than the ski slopes anyway. I'll talk to the others while we're away and devise a plan. What do you say?"

"Okay. Maybe we can go right after graduation, before we have to pack up for college." April did love the beach, the rolling ocean waves, the warm sand and bright sun. "Thanks for thinking of it, Kelli. You're a real friend."

Kelli beamed her a smile. "We'll call you from the ski lodge."

April nodded. "*Don't* break a leg."

Suddenly a male voice burst upon the two girls in the lounge. "There you are, April."

April looked up to see Chris Albright, the senior captain of their high-school soccer team. They'd been dating for a few months, ever since Christmas, but she hadn't expected him to pop into the hospital the day before spring break. She was glad she'd taken the time to put on her sweats and wasn't wearing a hospital gown.

"I couldn't find you in your room," Chris continued. "One of the nurses told me to check in here. You feeling better?"

Chris had caught her when she'd fainted in English class. Literally.

"Nothing to report," she said. He straddled the arm of her chair and took her hand in his. From the corner of her eye, April saw the patient who'd been ogling her lean forward. She turned her full attention to Chris. "I didn't think I'd see you until after the break."

"I can't go off and leave my girlfriend holed up in the hospital."

Kelli, who was out of Chris's line of vision, did an exaggerated swoon that made April giggle. Chris was the catch of their school. April was nuts about him, but she tried not to show it. Clingy girlfriends were a turnoff.

"What's so funny?" Chris asked.

"Nothing. I'm just glad to see you." She laced her fingers through his.

"What's up, Kelli?" Chris asked.

"I came to say goodbye too," Kelli told him. "Actually I was trying to persuade April to sneak away with me and leave her doctor a note about coming back after spring break."

"Makes sense to me," Chris said. "Have they told you anything yet?"

April told Chris what she'd told Kelli. Once again she omitted the information that she didn't want anyone to know. *The headaches can't be related,* she told herself. "So, I guess I'm stuck here until they complete all the tests," she finished aloud.

"What kind of doctor have you got?" Chris wanted to know.

"A neurologist." She leaned forward. "Personally, I think all this is a ploy to find out if I really have a brain."

Kelli rolled her eyes and Chris scoffed. "Right," he said. "You're on the dean's list every reporting period. I don't think brain loss is your problem."

They all laughed and April felt better. More than anything she wanted to be out of the hospital and back in the familiar world of school and friends and graduation plans. Graduation was only nine weeks away. *Stupid headaches!*

"Listen, I'd better run," Kelli said, standing. "I want to catch the train before rush hour."

"Thanks for visiting." April longed to be leaving with her friend.

"I'll call you." Kelli bent and hugged her goodbye. She whispered in April's ear, "I know three's a crowd," and darted out the door.

Chris eased into Kelli's vacated chair. "I miss you, April."

"I miss you too."

"You scared everybody when you blacked out in class."

"Did I ever thank you for catching me before I hit the floor?"

He glanced self-consciously around the room. "Is there any place less public than here?"

"My room."

"Let's go." He helped her to her feet.

The room spun and she clung to him. "It takes me a minute to get my balance whenever I change positions."

He looked concerned and put his arm around her waist. As they walked back to her room, April felt the gaze of the guy on the far side of the lounge area following them. She snuggled closer to Chris.

Once in the privacy of her room, Chris took her in his arms and kissed her. "I hate to leave you for a whole week." The soccer team was playing a tournament in Pennsylvania over the break.

"Go have a good time. But not too good a time."

He stayed for another hour before he kissed her goodbye.

Alone, she felt the gloom return. It would be another couple of hours before her parents would arrive. *Stop acting like a baby,* she told herself. *This isn't like before. You're seventeen now, not five.*

She was sitting up in her bed clicking through the TV channels with the remote control when someone rapped on her door. "Come in," she called.

The door slowly opened, and the boy from the rec room stood there. "Hi," he said with a sunny grin.

"Do I know you?" she asked.

"Mark Gianni." He held out his hand.

She took it cautiously. His grip was warm, his palm rough. He was tall and had curling dark brown hair and intense deep brown eyes. But Kelli had been right. He was thin, almost gaunt. "And you're here be-cause . . . ?" She allowed the sentence to trail.

"Because I want you to know that you're the most beautiful girl I've ever seen. And I thought I should introduce myself. I mean, we should get to know each other. Since you're the girl I intend to marry."

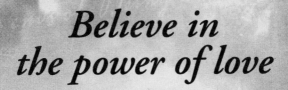